DOC DALTON,
DEMON Hunter

THOMAS M. MALAFARINA

**HELLBENDER
BOOKS**

an imprint of Sunbury Press, Inc.
Mechanicsburg, PA USA

an imprint of Sunbury Press, Inc.
Mechanicsburg, PA USA

For information about special discounts for bulk purchases, please contact Sunbury Press Orders Dept. at (855) 338-8359 or orders@sunburypress.com.

To request one of our authors for speaking engagements or book signings, please contact Sunbury Press Publicity Dept. at publicity@sunburypress.com.

FIRST HELLBENDER BOOKS EDITION: January 2025

Set in Adobe Garamond Pro | Interior design by Crystal Devine | Cover design by Lawrence Knorr | Edited by Lawrence Knorr.

Publisher's Cataloging-in-Publication Data
Names: Malafarina, Thomas M., author.
Title: Doc Dalton, demon hunter / Thomas M. Malafarina.
Description: First trade paperback edition. | Mechanicsburg, PA : Hellbender Books, 2025.
Summary: Join Doc Dalton In his adventures as he fights to seek and destroy the evil demons that threaten the souls of humanity.
Identifiers: ISBN 979-8-88819-288-7 (softcover).
Subjects: FICTION / Horror / Occult & Supernatural | FICTION / Science Fiction / Apocalyptic & Post-Apocalyptic.

Designed in the USA
0 1 1 2 3 5 8 13 21 34 55

For the Love of Books!

*This book, like all my books, is dedicated to
my amazing and lovely wife JoAnne,
who not only tolerates but supports all of my
often strange creative endeavors.*

INTRODUCTION

Welcome to the universe of *Doc Dalton, Demon Hunter*. It's a world where demons exist, unseen and unknown by the general public. Our hero, Doc Dalton, is a super cool dude whose job is to track down, confront, and destroy these monsters. This book is his story.

As a bit of history, in 2010, I wrote my second novel, *Burn Phone*, published September 9th, 2010, by Sunbury Press. Eight years later, on February 28, 2018, through Hellbender Books, a newly formed horror imprint of Sunbury Press, I reworked the novel, and Hellbender retitled it *Burner*. Then, they designed a new cover and released it under the new imprint.

Burner was the story of a businessman named Charles Wilson, who left home in rural Pennsylvania for the most important sales call of his career when he realized on the way to the Philadelphia airport that he had forgotten his cell phone. This critical device was his lifeline to the business world; over a thousand contacts were stored in its memory. Wilson's cell phone radically transformed him as a businessman and changed how he conducted business. Now, he found he simply could not function without it. In fact, if he was without his cell phone for even as little as an hour, Wilson felt completely cut off from the rest of the world, a world that provided him with a substantial income.

Charles decided that since he also had most of his contacts stored on his laptop computer, the best thing to do would be to have his wife overnight the phone to his hotel. In the interim, he would look to purchase a "burner phone"—street vernacular for a pre-paid cellular phone. Unfortunately, luck was not on Wilson's side as all the kiosks were closed at the airports, and when he arrived at his hotel, it was too late to make such a purchase. Charles was frustrated and berated himself for his foolishness. He inquired at the front desk for a place to buy a burner. A strange man sitting in the hotel lobby directed Charles to a dark alley, running along the side of the hotel. Unknown to Charles, the odd cell phone he eventually purchased at an even more bizarre antique store had the power to open a portal to Hell and bring forth demons to do his bidding. So begins Charles Wilson's Hellish journey. Without giving away any more of the book, let's say that lots of horrible things happen to many deserving people. *Burner* is an exercise in the adage that "Power corrupts, and absolute power corrupts absolutely."

The reason for this overview is because, throughout the past decade, I have often been asked to create a sequel to *Burner*. Unfortunately, I have never been inspired to write such a sequel. However, I had always thought I would do so if I had another idea for a completely different story and character and could pick up where *Burner* left off and use it in the new story. As such, this book is not a sequel to *Burner*, but it eventually incorporates the evil demon R. John Showalter from *Burner* into the story. It also makes historical references to *Burner's* content where necessary. So, in that regard, this novel is a "sort of" sequel without officially being a sequel.

Hopefully, those of you who still hunger for a *Burner* sequel will be satisfied, and those who have not read *Burner* will be inspired to do so after reading this story. So, sit back, relax, and enjoy *Doc Dalton, Demon Hunter*.

Thomas M. Malafarina
January 2025

PROLOGUE

The tall, lone figure stood silently at the mouth of the dark, dead-end alley. A cold, misty rain fell around him, collecting in the brim of his Australian black bull-hide leather Cessnock hat, where it trickled over the sides onto the shoulders of his knee-length, equally black leather trench coat. He liked black . . . a lot. He always wore black. As dark as the blackness of the void in his heart, a hole that could never be filled.

His piercing blue eyes scanned the almost impenetrable darkness, watching and waiting for why he was there. Moonlight shone across his back, reflecting off the glistening rivulets of rain running down the length of his coat and collecting in small puddles on the asphalt street below. Tiny drops of mist clung to his salt-and-pepper mustache and goatee and his long, graying mane of once-dark hair flowing from underneath his hat. He paid no mind. He was a man on a mission.

The man stood tall, well over six feet, his height accentuated further by his hat, long coat, and the silver-tipped steel-toe engineer boots visible below his black leather pants. His outfit did little to hide his broad shoulders and overly muscular body, which had been honed like the razor edge of a knife over the past ten years.

The man had more than his share of scars to testify to his struggle, including one that trailed from the side of his right eye down along his face, ending by his mouth. He had gotten that one at the start of it all. It had faded somewhat over the years, not that he cared one way or the other. He didn't need to impress anyone. On the third finger of his left hand, he wore a white-gold ring, his wedding band.

The big man stared down the narrow alley into the gloom, noticing the tall brick walls that bordered both sides. These ruins were all that remained of long-abandoned factory buildings. Their crumbling brick walls were covered with various forms of graffiti. Strange, cryptic gang symbols adorned them, with names of unknown taggers such as "Gizzmo 89" or "Wallman Joe." An abundance of crudely painted male and female sex organs were also painted on the brick. It was obvious from the flaked and faded condition of the artwork that it had been done many years earlier, and no one had been down this alley in a very long time.

The windows in the old buildings had gone through the decades-old evolution from metal-framed, white-washed glass panes to boarded-over plywood to their current empty black state, resembling the vacant eye sockets of dozens of ancient rotting skulls. The man cautiously scanned those holes with his peripheral vision as he focused on the street ahead. He knew the street was where the threat would originate. That was how it always was, but it never hurt to be overly cautious, especially when walking into an alley resembling a shooting gallery in a bad 1980s video game. He knew it was always important to be aware of potential ambush points.

Although supernatural threats could come in an unlimited number of different shapes and sizes and from any plane of existence, there was also the human threat. This type of attack could come not only from regular humans out to do evil; it could be initiated by those living minions of the damned who dutifully served their demonic masters. This was a fact the man knew well, yet what he didn't know at this time was he would forget that important bit of knowledge in a few days, and it would almost cost him his life and his immortal soul.

A faint vibration began at the center of his chest. There was no need to look down; he knew what he would see because he knew what was causing the sensation. It was the amulet. The relic was sensing an arrival, as it never failed to do. A slight crimson illumination glowed below his field of vision, coming from the ruby eyes embedded in the large, flat silver skull hanging from the heavy silver chain around his neck. Over many years, it had become as much a part of him as any of his body parts. Next to his wedding band, it was the most precious thing he owned.

The piece had been hand-crafted centuries earlier, created in the same image as its evil counterpart. That other medallion was a doppelganger, an unholy relic that had existed since the dawn of humanity. Although fashioned thousands of years later, his amulet was constructed to be used only as a force for good. The surface of the talisman had been painstakingly etched with a myriad of symbols, each selected from a particular ancient scroll, chosen to work in concert, both for the wearer's protection and to act as an early warning system, which it was presently doing.

As the big man stood in silence, he felt the earth begin to tremble under his feet, and out in the darkness, he could hear the asphalt begin to crack, bubble, and rise. It split a few seconds later like an overripe watermelon baking in the hot sun. A pale yellowish light glowed in the center of the street, spreading thinly toward him. The asphalt groaned and rose like a fresh puckering scar in the earth. It split open, and bright red molten lava spilled over the edges of the widening crevasse as vast clouds of billowing smoke and steam rose skyward. An all too familiar yet disgusting, stomach-churning stench flowed from the void, a mixture of sulfur, feces, and decomposing meat.

As the crack widened and the earth rumbled, the crimson and yellow light became brighter as white-hot flames shot upward. Any remaining rain puddles instantly turned to steam, adding to the already present fog and creating a thicker, eerie mist that quickly permeated the area. The light from the ever-growing wall of flames provided a gut-wrenching view of the horror spewing from deep within the rising vapor.

The man was not disturbed by what he saw. He understood the purpose of theatrics, such as he now witnessed. It was always the same, a larger-than-life production; its goal was to intimidate the observer, make him tremble with fear, and have him pray for the salvation of his immortal soul. However, the big man wouldn't be discouraged; it was not his nature. Instead of fleeing in terror, he advanced slowly toward the flaming wound in the earth, ready to face this challenge as he had done countless times before.

From inside the glowing split in the earth, long brownish-green snake-like tentacles emerged, whipping about frenetically, searching for any living thing within their grasp, the mouths at the ends of these serpentine monstrosities gleaming with multiple rows of razor-sharp teeth. Just above these mouths were two antennae with bulbous eyeballs. Their purpose was obvious; they were searching, looking for him.

He thought of these aberrations as scouts, but sacrificial lambs might be a more accurate description. They always came first. They were never a match for his skills, yet time after time, they came. Regardless, he never became overconfident or let down his guard. Perhaps their purpose was to tire him, or maybe they were sent hoping that someday, the odds were, one of them might get past his defenses and do the job they were created for. Or maybe there was some other, more sinister reason these creatures always led the vanguard, something he had not yet imagined. No matter the reason, they were here, and they were here to kill him and take his soul to Hell.

One of the whipping creatures stopped and looked directly at the man. It had found its quarry and, having done so, released a high-pitched keening whine of satisfaction. Soon, the remaining dozen or more tentacle creatures were likewise focused on the man's direction, becoming a chorus of shrieking Hell-spawned choir boys, resembling a cluster of spitting cobras dancing in the air before him. However, these creatures were much more deadly, having the cobra's speed but the size and girth of boa constrictors.

If one of these behemoths managed to wrap itself around him, he wouldn't have to worry about their deadly teeth. The monsters' fiery, scaly skin would burn through his leather clothing like paper and liquefy his flesh from his bones in milliseconds. The creatures suddenly stopped screaming simultaneously and tensed for a moment. Then, as was typical, they attacked.

The man stood stock still, waiting for the right moment, his arms positioned at the ready, his long coat opened, revealing two leather sheaths, one on each side of his thick belt. As the tentacle creatures attacked, the man's two arms moved faster than any human eye could see, each gripped tightly to a handle, withdrawing two gleaming silver Katana blades.

As he pulled them from their scabbards, the man crossed them in the air, severing the head from the closest serpentine monster, sending it flying back into the flaming pit from which it came, its body crashing to the ground. As its decapitated corpse flipped and flopped helplessly, a deep yellow pus-colored goo that passed for the creature's blood spurted onto the asphalt, where it burst into flames, melting the blacktop and creating dozens of small fiery puddles. After a few moments of thrashing, the thing shriveled up, dissolving into a pond of foul-smelling ooze.

Before the demonic viper wholly dissolved, more of the wretched creatures attacked, each bent on destroying the man in the black coat. As these other monsters made their moves, he dispatched them one by one, spinning and whirling about with more grace than a man his size should possess. His gleaming swords, like buzzsaws, became a deadly blur, slicing and dismembering among the cries of agony from the serpentine monsters. Soon, the alley was littered with the dead and dissolving remains of the horrible creatures. The flaming pools of disintegrating flesh slowly began to die and eventually burn out, although the enormous, glowing, stinking gash in the alley remained, as the man knew it would.

The man snapped his blades downward, flicking the remnants of the creatures' burning flesh to the asphalt. He held his glistening swords before his face, admiring the hundreds of etched symbols covering their surface. Like those on his amulet, each blade bore hand-carved glyphs etched at the exact location, position, and orientation to make them the most effective at harming the forces of evil and protecting the swords from the blazing fires of Hell. As such, they always did their job with incredible efficiency.

He backed up a few steps, returning to his original place near the open end of the alley, looking at the baking, bubbling mess and watching the flaming chasm with anticipation. The rain had stopped, and the steaming mist was dissipating. The man knew this was not the end of things by any means. There would be more; there always was more. This simple attack by these sacrificial demonic serpents was not why his amulet led him here. He was confident it was only the opening act of a much more dangerous performance of the damned.

He didn't have long to wait. Within a few seconds, the crack in the street widened further, and the skull medallion against his chest began to vibrate and glow with much more severity. At the widest point of the crack near the center, two monstrous hands emerged, one on each side, grabbing onto the molten blacktop. They pushed against the asphalt, widening the opening. The appendages were unaffected by the flames or the bubbling hot melting tar, their leathery flesh gripping the asphalt as it was liquefied and then enlarged.

Those hands were huge, over two feet wide, coated in gray-green flesh with long gnarled fingers equipped with deadly talons. The hands gleamed with some slimy napalm-like coating, which oozed and slid down along their lengths. Like a feted pig stile, a new stench was added to the revolting concoction. The man recognized that foul stink and knew it was coming from this approaching creature. To make things even more disgusting, the man likened the arrival of this latest Hell-born creature to an image of the earth giving birth to the horrible monster.

Once the hands had gained purchase, a creature emerged from the fiery pit. First, its hideous head could be partially seen amid the growing smoke and flames. It had large ram-like horns curving back from its skull among a thick mane of long, greasy black hair and bulging, hateful eyes. The pig-like snout, typical of these lesser demons, sniffed the air, trying to identify its prey. Soon, its entire body had made its way up and onto the asphalt, where it rose to its gargantuan size.

The demon was beyond horrifying, standing more than ten feet tall with arms almost equal to that in length, dangling down practically to the ground. Like its hands, the creature's feet had long toes equipped with similar deadly talons. The monster was naked, gleaming with a shiny coating of translucent snot-like ooze; the man couldn't help but think of it as Hell's afterbirth. The monster's flesh was covered with hundreds of painful-looking open weeping sores. Its skin was a roadmap of scars, suggesting the beast had previously been tortured regularly.

A massive gut and troll-like man-boobs hung from its scarred and blistered chest. The monster was most definitely male, as could be seen by the gigantic thick phallus, which dangled between its legs, practically reaching the ground. The member looked to be the creature's most painful appendage of all as it was skewered with what appeared to be thousands of long needle-like piercings, studs, rings, and razor wire. Whatever atrocities this creature had committed in life, it was most definitely paying for its sins in death.

As the large man watched in curious silence, molten rock and flames began to swirl along the smoking surface of the asphalt, shaping into a gigantic sword. It was a massive scimitar, more than six feet long, with a blade at least five inches wide at the hilt and almost a foot wide at the business end. Flames licked up and down its glowing edge. Without bending to retrieve the flaming sword, the creature extended one of its massive hands, and the handle jumped into the monster's grasp. Then, another blade formed like the first and found its way into the creature's other hand.

The heinous beast opened its horrible slit of a mouth, revealing a cavernous maw filled with hundreds of razor-sharp fangs. More than a foot long, its serpentine tongue darted in and out of its mouth. Blood dripped from open slices on the monster's tongue where it came into contact with those deadly fangs. This demon, as terrifying as it might be, was a study of horror and agony. Then again, these demonic minions always were. And why not? After all, suffering was the very definition of Hell. The beast stared menacingly at the man in black for a moment through sunken, red-rimmed bulging eyes; then it spoke in a low guttural voice barely discernable as English.

"Hathaway Everett Dalton, I presume. You are also known as Doc, I am told. I have come for you, Doc Dalton," the beast proclaimed.

Dalton stood his ground silently waiting, his hands crossed in front of him, each one still on the handles of his blades. He studied the pathetic creature before him with disgust mixed with pity. No doubt, the beast must have been offered some minor reprieve from the constant agony and tortures of Hell if it agreed to take on this assignment. As intimidating and monstrous as this beast might appear, Dalton knew the demon would be no match for his skills. He would slay this demon as he had slain so many before it. Dalton had no choice. Yet he felt somewhat sorry for the monster because it chose to risk destruction at Dalton's hands to an eternity of torture. Then the beast spoke again.

"Doc, is it? Why do they call you Doc? You don't look like much of a doctor to me."

Dalton didn't respond. He knew what the monster was doing. It was trying to throw him off balance, to taunt him into being off his game with that annoying "Doc" barb. The creature had been well-coached and had known that most people questioned Doc's nickname, an inquiry which often annoyed him, especially those who insisted on the old Bugs Bunny favorite, "What's up Doc?" But not today. Because, as always, today, he was focused.

The creature spoke again, "Well, Mr. Doc, but no doctor, Dalton, it's only fitting that you should know the name of the one who will kill you, don't you agree? Please allow me to introduce myself as that song says. I am known in Hell as 'Fraggzzorr the Destroyer.' It is a name that strikes fear into the hearts of even the evilest of demons. I have withstood unimaginable torture and agony and have provided equal measures to others. When I was still alive and human, I was known as Edmund Carlton Blake or, as some people of lesser intellect called me, Baby Butcher Blake. Perhaps you have heard of me."

Dalton knew that name very well. Edmund C. Blake had been a nineteenth-century madman who had raped, killed, and dismembered more than twenty small children in his home and then cannibalized their remains. It was suddenly no surprise to Dalton why this wretched creature had been tormented so severely in Hell. Any pity Dalton previously had for the beast was gone.

"Ah, I can see by your expression you have heard of me and most likely know of my many exploits. I assume you also heard how disrespectfully the populace treated me in life. What a shame those moronic yokels didn't better understand the finer points of what it took to be me."

Dalton recalled what he had read once regarding Blake's demise. On the night of Blake's death, the killer had been dragged from his home by a mob of townspeople who beat him almost to death before hanging him from a tall oak, where he dangled gagging until he eventually died. Afterward, they left the body suspended so birds and insects could all share his flesh. Several days later, what was left of the body slipped from the noose and landed in a broken heap where ground scavengers finished it.

Hell had claimed Blake's soul as it had done with countless other damned creatures before him. By the looks of the wretched beast, Blake had been tortured in ways unimaginable to any sane person. The scars showed that, as did the piercings. Blake's soul had been transformed into this hideous demonic incarnation of the degenerate child murderer. Now, that monster stood before him.

This would be Hell's latest feeble attempt to kill Dalton and possess his soul. He chuckled to himself, wondering why he had to waste his time with the likes of this pathetic creature. If that was the best they could come up with, then the rulers of Hell were not very creative. Although Dalton typically didn't interact verbally with these demons, he decided it might be appropriate to do some trash-talking himself.

Dalton sneered and said, "I love what you've done with yourself, Blake. Hell looks good on you. I'm sure it's an improvement over your previous looks. I read that you frequented brothels and bordellos in life because you were so heinous that no respectable woman would consider coming anywhere near you. In all the reports, you were described as physically repugnant. Well, if women thought you were ugly before, they should see you now. But then again, you probably wouldn't care what grown women thought of you since you gave up sluts a long time ago in favor of little children, didn't you, you sick bastard?"

"How dare you defame me! You don't know me! You're like the rest of them. You will never be able to understand my needs and desires. You consider yourself much too superior for that, don't you, Doc Dalton? You're simply too boring, too normal. With you, everything is either right or wrong, either black or white. Is that not so? There is never anything in between, never a gray area."

Dalton smiled sardonically and said, "Well, how inconsiderate of me for being so normal. Forgive me all to Hell, pun intended. I'm sorry, I can't appreciate your raping, murdering, and cannibalizing little kids. I suppose that's just one of my many flaws. Please accept my humble apology, Scraggswhore."

"That's Fraggzzorr . . . Fraggzzorr the Destroyer."

"Oh yeah, that's right. Sorry. Ok, Fraggalosoreass, how's about you and me get all this over with," Dalton said, taunting, "We both know why you're here and what you want, so how's about we get rockin' and rollin' already?"

"It will be my pleasure to slice you to pieces with my mighty swords of fire, then drag your pleading soul back with me into the stinking bowels of Hell, where you will spend eternity in agonizing torture at the feet of my master."

"Blah, blah blah, yadda, yadda, yadda. You demons all spew the same crap. And you call me boring? Well, Fragspore, I hate to burst your pustule, but your so-called master will have to pucker up and smooch my lily-white backside because I won't be goin' anywhere with you today or tomorrow or, for that matter, any time."

"Then prepare to die, Doc Dalton, you worthless insect!" The monster shouted as it lumbered up the alley toward Dalton, its blazing swords dripping lava as they spun like helicopter blades. Dalton remained still, once again waiting for the exact right moment.

When the creature was almost upon him, Dalton drew his Katana blades while simultaneously sliding below the monster's whirring swords along the creature's right side. The Demon passed overhead, unable to stop his forward trajectory because of his sheer size. As it did, Dalton sliced off most of the demon's dangling pin-pierced member and simultaneously cut into one of the beast's legs.

Steaming green slime oozed from the monster's open wounds as it let out a series of agonized howls and crashed to the asphalt below. The gelatinous liquid flowed, covering the ground and causing the blacktop to bubble. The severed three-foot-long remnants of what was once the monster's most prized possession slithered away like a wounded baby python, diving back into the stinking crack in the earth.

Dalton had returned to a standing position, staying as far from the fiery opening in the alley and the wounded demon as possible. He hoped the creature would likewise crawl into the crack and follow his severed member back to Hell. However, despite its wounds, the monster was not finished. As it attempted to get up again, Dalton shot forward and lowered his blades to decapitate the creature, but a block thwarted his attack from one of the enormous flaming swords. The blades crashed together with an ear-ringing clang.

Even though the swords had only touched briefly, Dalton could feel the heat from the Hell-formed weapon crawling up his blades. Even the intricately carved glyphs could do little to fight off the scorching Hellfire. Backing away momentarily, he kept hold of the handles as the swords cooled to normal. This gave the creature time to rise slowly to a standing position. As it did, Dalton couldn't help but notice that the monster was now only slightly favoring its wounded leg.

Then, to Dalton's shock and disgust, the monster's severed phallus had not only cauterized itself but had begun to regenerate right before his eyes and did so very quickly. Within seconds, the demon-dong was back to its original length and girth, in all its phallic glory, minus the piercings. Likewise, the slice in the creature's leg had healed as well.

The beast roared in anger, obviously surprised by the speed and cunning Dalton, a mere mortal, seemed to possess. For a moment, the demon wondered whether it would successfully kill this human. After all, many had failed before him. But he was confident he could crush this man. The few strikes the human managed to land were minor nicks that must have been nothing more than lucky glances. This human maggot had no idea just how powerful a demon he was.

"That was a good one, Dalton. I suppose I'll have to credit you that much. Very good, indeed. But I think I'll call that a lucky shot. However, I won't give you such an opportunity again, human. You are mine now, Doc Dalton, or should I say, my master's? Oh, the pain and torture he will show you will be agony beyond your comprehen . . ."

But the demon couldn't finish its sentence, as one of Dalton's Katana blades had been thrust through its neck. Dalton pulled the blade free along with much of the demon's throat. The monster tried to scream, but all that came out was a watery gurgling sound. The devil dropped its swords and grabbed for its ravaged throat, trying desperately to keep any more of its essence from spilling down the front of his bulbous stomach.

"Less talk, more rock," Dalton said.

Greenish brown globs of stinking goo poured from the demon's open throat, where a massive wound of flapping flesh dangled. Dalton knew he couldn't waste time, or the beast would regenerate itself again. He twirled around in circles, spinning his Katana blades like a fan. They quickly found the still-tattered remnants of the monster's throat and separated its head from its neck.

The head flew through the air, eventually hitting the ground and rolling into the flaming crack in the alley. The monster's body stood on wobbly legs for a second or so before falling backward and landing on the asphalt with a loud thud. As Dalton watched, a dozen or more of those strange snake-like creatures shot out of the opening, looking about wildly. But this time, they weren't there for Dalton; they had come to reclaim the remains of his latest vanquished demon.

They did their job quickly and efficiently, biting deep into the flesh and painstakingly dragging the giant corpse back toward the fiery pit. The two giant swords transformed back to burning magma as they melted and flowed harmlessly into the crack in the earth. Within a few minutes, the body disappeared over the edge and from sight. All the serpents retreated down into the abyss except for the largest creature. Its head moved back and forth in its cobra-like dance, never taking its antennae-mounted eyes off Dalton.

It didn't move its mouth, yet still, Dalton heard a voice inside his mind, a half-human, half-serpentine hissing whisper.

"Maybe not thisssss time, Dalton, but sssssoon, very sssssoon."

"I don't think so," Dalton replied with his mind. Then he heard another voice in his mind, one he knew very well, but it couldn't possibly be because his beloved wife had died over ten years earlier.

"Doc? Honey, it's Audrey. Help me, please. I don't want to be here. They keep hurting me and doing unimaginable things to me. They won't let me go. Please, Baby, come down and rescue me."

The hissing voice returned, "That'ssss right, Dalton, we have your precioussass wife'sss sssssoul, and we've been torturing it for a decade. Why don't you sssssstep a little clossssser and we'll let you ssssssee her? You want to ssssssee her, don't you? Ssssstep a little closssser."

"Nice try, fang face, but I know better. My wife was as close to an earthbound angel as any living human could possibly be. I know she's in Heaven now and waiting for me. I mean, seriously, when are you clowns going to give up on all those feeble attempts at playing with my emotions by lying and tempting me? That crap might have worked a few millennia ago with stupid peasants, but it doesn't fly nowadays. So how about you get out of here before I slice you up into a million itsy bitsy worms."

The snake creature repeated, "We may not have gotten you thisss time, Dalton, but ssssomeday ssssoon."

Then the snake creature vanished into the pit along with that horrible voice. As he stood in silence, the flaming slit in the street closed itself back up as the tar began to cool, returning to a normal state.

Dalton turned to walk away, then looked back and said to the dark, empty street, "Not next time either, maggot breath. I'll be ready as always." Then he walked out of the alley onto the main street and disappeared into the shadows.

CHAPTER 1

The steaming hot water from the shower felt incredible on Dalton's aching muscles as tendrils of the healing liquid ran down over his scarred and tattoo-covered body. Like the glyphs carved into his medallion and sword, his body art was carefully designed to provide Dalton with maximum protection against the powers of the underworld.

As the water flowed down the shower drain, its cleansing power seemed to take all of the day's troubles with it, leaving Dalton feeling much better. A good hot shower always made him feel refreshed and new. It also provided him with a place to contemplate life and plan his next strategy. Although he was physically large, strong, imposing, and fearless, he was also wise and more than a little cautious. Hunting and destroying demons tended to bring that out in a man.

Dalton was thinking about the passage of time and his age, not for the first time. It had been more than a decade since he had left his safe and secure reality to find himself fighting monsters more horrid than most people's worst nightmares. Whenever he took the time to think of such things, it all seemed surrealistic, as if he was watching a movie about someone else's life. He had never imagined his life taking the course it had taken. That world seemed like a lifetime ago; in essence, it was since his old life had ended shortly before the new one had begun.

Now, all these years later, the life he had chosen, or more accurately, the life which had chosen him, was taking its toll on his aging body in the form of wear and tear. It's not that Dalton was elderly or weak by any means. He was in excellent physical condition for a man his age. Still, he was no longer considered a proverbial spring chicken either.

Whatever the case, he always found the hot water physically and mentally therapeutic. Dalton felt he did his best thinking in the shower, as he suspected many people did. What he was currently thinking about, and not for the first time, was what his end game might be. He questioned where his life was going. He had accidentally fallen into this demon-hunting thing with no real direction. And now, more than a decade later, he had no more of a plan for his life than he had previously.

Then again, could he really consider himself a demon hunter? It wasn't like he tried to track down and destroy demons. That's the sort of offensive maneuvering a true demon hunter would use. Dalton was much more defensive in his demon slaying. The denizens of Hell came looking for him almost all the time. Dalton knew why, and that thing always stood in his way whenever he thought of hanging up his blades.

He could never stop because he had been marked; Sensei Chang had said so. That, unfortunately, meant he would be destroying demons for the rest of his life as Chang had done. He had no choice. Someday, he, too, would be an old man forced to confront the forces of Hell. Would he have to find another warrior to train to take his place? So many questions.

Dalton finished his shower, not finding any philosophical answers to his life questions, but at least he felt better. He dried himself off, put on his undershorts, and lay in his bed under his covers. He knew sleep would be slow coming, even though he was physically and mentally exhausted. As he lay in bed, Dalton unconsciously turned the wedding band on the third finger of his left hand. He thought as he often did about his beloved late wife, Audrey, and the events that brought him to where he was now.

CHAPTER 2

Audrey had been the one true love of Dalton's life. They had met during his senior year in college and married a year later. The couple had never been blessed with children, which saddened them but never affected their love for each other. They had been considering adoption right before Aubrey was diagnosed with cancer. A year later, she was gone. Thinking about his life's twists and turns since then, Dalton realized it was for the best that they had been childless.

After his wife's death, Dalton had been as lost as a rudderless boat in the middle of a raging sea. He was angry about the dreaded cancer, which had ravaged and taken her at such a young age. He thought of how the disease had robbed her of her youth and beauty, leaving a wretched hollow remnant of the woman she had once been. Even up to the end, Audrey had fought hard to beat it, and Dalton had been by her side the whole time, encouraging her every step along the way.

He had wanted to strike out at anyone or anything, to make the pain in his heart disappear. But that was the problem with an illness like Audrey's cancer; there was no one to blame or strike. Dalton would have done anything to fill the empty hole her death had created inside him during that time. But nothing could ease his grief. They say time heals all wounds, but Dalton disagreed. The only thing time seemed to do was dull his senses and cloud his memories, but his wounds never healed, and the pain never went away.

Dalton had eventually quit his job, not that it would have mattered much. He had been on an unpaid leave of absence for the previous six months to care for Audrey. He suspected if he had returned to work, they might have tolerated him for a few months out of sympathy for the death of his wife. However, eventually, they would have laid him off. There had been an economic recession then, and he found his services were no longer needed.

He sold the only home he and his wife had ever shared at a below-market price, but Dalton didn't care. He didn't care about much of anything. He put the money from the house sale and Audrey's life insurance into a bank account and essentially forgot about it. He started living on the streets among the outcasts of society, the homeless, the destitute, and the unwanted. In that world of unknown lost souls, he could disappear and blend in with the rest of the nameless, faceless street people.

As far as Dalton was concerned, his life had ended when Audrey died. He was nothing more than a hollow shell, a dead man walking. Day after day, he awoke, stumbled through another meaningless day, and slept again. His life was over, or at least he thought it was over, until one day, everything suddenly changed.

CHAPTER 3

Dalton recalled that fateful night, the one that changed his life forever. He had been sitting alone in his "home," a makeshift tent under a highway overpass. All around him were dozens of other homeless street people, each with their own shelters constructed of various salvaged materials. Dalton's tent, for example, was relatively weather-proof as it was built from an old canvas painting tarpaulin he had found in a dumpster. Most of the others were less secure, made of old blankets and cardboard boxes. It was obvious that some of Dalton's neighbors were envious of his digs. There was apparently a pecking order, even among the refuse of society.

However, no one in the encampment ever bothered Dalton or touched his meager possessions. This was likely not just because of his size but also because of the hostile, angry, unapproachable expression he always wore. Most street folks were dealing with one type of mental disorder or another. But no matter how severe their affliction, they were wise enough to steer clear whenever they encountered someone of Dalton's size and his apparently foul disposition. And that suited Dalton just fine.

On occasion, Dalton wondered what sort of mental disorder he might have. Did grief and a broken heart count as a mental illness? Perhaps not, but he understood the depression he was suffering from in the wake of his loss certainly couldn't be considered mentally healthy. Dalton knew he needed something to distract him and hopefully break him out of this world of never-ending heartache and suffering.

Yet strangely, part of him didn't want that. Part of him wanted to suffer, needed to suffer. Perhaps it was more than grief; maybe it was what Dalton had heard referred to as survivor's guilt. He was alive, while his precious Audrey was dead. These depressing, maudlin thoughts made up his typical day. The day he had just lived through had been no different. Another day had come and gone without him even realizing it. He knew he had been sitting in his tent under the highway, staring into space and thinking of all he had lost. He might have dozed off then but couldn't remember doing so. Now, wide awake, he would face another dark and lonely night. That was when he heard a strange noise.

He bent down from his sitting position, looked out through the open front flap of his tent, and saw something going on up the street from the encampment. A glowing light came from an alley and shone onto the cross street. He could hear moaning and the sound of a struggle, perhaps several people fighting.

Usually, Dalton would never have bothered to investigate such a thing. One important thing he learned from the street people was not to look for trouble, as it was always waiting for him. For a moment, Dalton considered ignoring the situation, minding his own business, and turning in for the night. But that night, he wasn't sleepy and was suddenly surprised to find himself more than a little curious about that glowing light and those strange sounds. So, he left the security of his tent and headed toward the source of his curiosity.

As he approached the entrance to the side street, Dalton heard loud shouting and what sounded like fighting coming from the alley. In his world among the homeless, such things were daily occurrences, and he knew the sounds well. Dalton tried to see down the alley but discovered the bright light shining out of the side street, which was so bright he could hardly make out what was happening. When he finally could focus, he couldn't believe his eyes.

He saw great flames rising, impossibly shooting upward from a large crack in the ground. He wondered what could possibly be going on in there. He thought again that maybe he should return to his tent and forget about whatever was happening. Then he saw something that made him change his mind, something which would, unbeknownst to him, eventually change his life as he knew it forever.

An old man was lying on the ground not far from the flaming fissure, and he appeared to be unconscious or dead. As Dalton got closer, he saw long snake-like tendrils squirming out of the flaming crack in the earth. They were grayish-green in color and coated with a burning gelatinous material, reminding Dalton of old videos he had seen of the military using napalm to exfoliate the jungles of Vietnam.

He couldn't believe what he was seeing. It was impossible, like something out of one of his worst nightmares. He glanced back toward his tent under the overpass, expecting to see himself sound asleep there, but he could see through the open flap that his shelter was empty. Dalton couldn't comprehend how, but somehow, what he saw was all impossibly true.

The tendril-like things were creeping toward the unconscious man. Dalton knew he had to find some way to help the old-timer, assuming the man was still alive. Just then, the wounded man opened his eyes and jumped to his feet with surprising speed. Dalton could see the man was Asian. The old man began fighting back to the best of his ability, with more energy than Dalton thought possible for a man of his advanced years.

However, it was clear the old man had been weakened by these strange attackers and appeared somewhat disoriented. The man cut down several of the tendrils closest to him using long, thin swords. Dalton had seen similar swords in Asian karate movies and knew them to be called Katana blades. Despite the old timer's best efforts, more creatures soon followed. Dalton stopped trying to comprehend what he was seeing. He figured he'd have to sort it all out later. Right now, the old guy obviously needed his help.

Dalton had no weapons, not that he would have known much about using them anyway. What little he understood about weapons and self-defense he had gotten from watching TV and movies. He wasn't totally without at least some small bit of experience, as he had been in a brawl or two during his youth and still hoped he could handle himself in a scuffle. But this wasn't a street brawl; these were bizarre, deadly creatures, the likes of which Dalton had never seen before. This was a life-and-death struggle.

He looked around for something he could throw like a rock, if for no other reason than to distract the monsters long enough to give the man some time to recover fully. He saw nothing he could use. Dalton could see the old man swinging those thin metal blades through the air and cutting some of the serpents to pieces, but there were just too many of them, and they kept coming at him.

Then Dalton looked to his right and saw four metal trashcans lined up behind one of the buildings, which backed into the alley. Maybe there would be something in one of those cans he could use. As he lifted the first lid, he noticed that the trash can wasn't one of the flimsy modern cans but an old-style can made of heavy-duty galvanized steel.

The lids looked like they had been run over by many trucks over the years, as they were smashed flat with tattered and broken edges. They were so flat they looked ridiculous sitting atop the can, scarcely able to cover the opening. Dalton almost cut his hand on a sharp metal edge, picking one of them up. This suddenly gave him an idea. Holding the first lid and finding a safe place on its edge, Dalton gripped it like a Frisbee, then hurled the cover into the cluster of serpents.

"Take that, you stinkin' slimeballs!" Dalton shouted as he watched the trashcan lid fly smoothly through the air and cleave more than six of the creatures in half as cleanly as any sword might do. He grabbed two more damaged covers and repeated his actions as more monsters were destroyed with equal efficiency. The old man continued to cut down the serpents with his swords, but Dalton could see he was weak and on the verge of collapsing.

As he was ready to throw the last lid, Dalton saw a long tubular piece of metal lying near the trashcans. It appeared to be a discarded conduit, perhaps removed from one of the old buildings. It was about five feet long with a ninety-degree elbow on one end while the other was roughly broken, leaving a sharp edge.

"Not perfect, but it'll have to do," Dalton thought as he grabbed the elbow like the hilt of a sword with his right hand and grabbed the handle of a smashed trashcan lid in his left hand, using it as a shield. He advanced into the alley, toward the flaming crack in the earth, swinging the makeshift blade like an ancient Roman warrior.

The old man stumbled backward from the fight, dropped his swords, and fell to the ground, collapsing from exhaustion and passing out. Not taking time to think of the potential futility of his actions, Dalton charged the snake things and managed to destroy two of them with the sharp end of his pipe before it became hot from their blazing bodies and began to glow red.

Dalton dropped the pipe, his hands burning, unable to hold onto it. He threw his last trashcan lid and took out another of the monsters before the metal cover burst into flames and melted. Then, several remaining monsters turned all their attention to Dalton and squirmed toward him. He saw the old man's two blades lying near his prone body and bent down to pick them up.

He felt something he had never felt before as he stood holding the swords. Strength began to flow like electricity through his body, and any uncertainty he might have experienced was replaced by complete confidence. He knew these remaining creatures, hideous as they were, would be no match for him as long as he held the blades.

Dalton attacked the flaming snakes, swinging the blades with a skill he never knew he possessed, and as he chopped them to pieces, they screamed and howled in agony. As their severed body parts landed on the asphalt, they wriggled for a second before disappearing in a puff of smoke. Some remains slid back into the fiery pit and vanished from sight.

When the last one of the creatures was killed, the ground began to tremble as the crack in the earth closed itself up, and the flames died to nothing. Within a few moments, the street had returned to being a street once again, and the alley was thrown back into darkness, save for what illumination the evening's moon provided.

Dalton felt a warm trickle of something running down his face. He lifted his palm and felt a thin line of raised flesh tender to the touch. It started next to his right eye, and as his fingers gingerly followed the line of puckered flesh, he felt the wound ending at the right side of his mouth.

"Burned," Dalton said with disappointment, "That's gonna leave a mark. Those damned things got me somehow. I guess I'm lucky; that's all they got."

Dalton checked the old man and saw he was still alive but unconscious. He lifted the man over his shoulders and carried him out of the alley.

CHAPTER 4

Dalton awoke in his shelter the following morning with the strange feeling of being watched. This sort of paranoia was expected when living among homeless people who were always watchful and untrusting of others. When you carry all your worldly possessions in a backpack or shopping cart, you tend to guard them with your life. But this feeling seemed different, somehow less general, more personal.

As his eyes focused, Dalton saw an old Asian man sitting cross-legged in his tent, staring at him. The man was mostly bald but had long white hair around the rim of his head, pulled back into a braid-like ponytail. He had a long Fu Manchu mustache and a goatee. The man's eyes projected knowledge and intelligence, suggesting this simple old man had seen a lot in his many years on Earth. In his exhaustion, Dalton had forgotten about the previous night's encounter in the alley and the old man. At first, Dalton was unsure what to say since he had never found himself in such a situation. He decided the best way to deal with this was to approach the problem head-on.

Dalton said, "Good morning, Sir. How are you? You know . . . how are you feeling?"

The old man smiled, revealing several empty spaces where teeth had previously resided. Then he said, "I am fine, thank you.

Or I suppose I should say thank you for saving my life." Dalton was surprised by the man's almost flawless English, with scarcely any noticeable accent whatsoever. And what had he just said about Dalton saving his life?

Dalton was caught a bit off guard, "I . . . I didn't save your life, old-timer; as I remember things, I just offered you a little assistance. You were doing fine without me."

The old man shook his almost bald head. Wispy strands of long white hair fluttered about as if caught in a breeze. "No, my young friend, that is not true; I know I would have been slain last night had you not shown up when you did. You were quite resourceful. I must admit, you were a natural, much more so than I could have imagined."

Dalton hesitated momentarily, then asked, "What exactly happened in that alley last night? When we got back here, I was exhausted and collapsed just like you did. Now, I can't figure out how much of what happened was real and how much might be part of a bad dream I may have had after falling asleep. It sure seemed real enough at the time, but in hindsight, so much was like a bad nightmare. So, now, I'm not so sure what actually did happen."

The old man remained silent.

Dalton said, "I mean, I know I helped you last night; I can recall that much. But it was more likely that you were being attacked by thugs, regular street punks. You know, the kind of scumbags that target older citizens, no offense intended. The way I figure it, I must have helped you fight them off, and then I brought you back here. In my exhausted state, when I fell asleep, the thugs in my dreams were transformed into . . . well, into something else. Yeah, that makes sense. I'm pretty sure that's what must have happened."

Finally, the old man stared at Dalton with what seemed to be all-seeing, all-knowing eyes and replied, "There were no thugs, no criminals, and no dreams. What you believe you saw was exactly what you did see, my large friend. It was not part of anything so explainable as a simple nightmare. Listen closely to what I tell you because it is more important than you realize. Last night in that alley, you fought off demons, sent forth from the deepest bowels of Hell for one purpose: to hunt me down, kill me, and take my soul back to their master."

Dalton hesitated momentarily, trying to absorb everything the old man told him. He was beginning to realize the old guy was either crazy or this was some kind of joke, and this character was just yanking his crank. He asked in a tone of disbelief, "Demons, you say? Real, live pitchfork-carrying little devils? You can't be serious."

"Of course, I'm serious, young man, as you should be as well. You were there last night, no matter what you choose to believe or not believe. You saw the monsters from Hell, fought them, and drove them back into Hell using your natural skills. By doing so, you also saved my life. I was weakened by their attack, and if not for you, I would be dead, and my immortal soul would be in Satan's hands."

Dalton couldn't wrap his brain around what this nice but crazy old man told him. Maybe this guy had Dementia or something and had escaped from some old folks home. Or worse, he might be like the rest of these street people, most of whom were crazy as bed bugs.

Dalton said, "Look, Pops, this is way too bizarre for me to accept. Demons from Hell coming out of the ground to try to kill you and steal your soul? You have to admit, that's a strange pill for me to try and swallow. I'm not nearly as wackadoodle as most of the crazies out here in this world. But, ok. For the sake of discussion, let's say that I buy into all this hocus-pocus demon-ocus baloney . . . which, by the way, I don't. Let's say you actually were attacked by demons from Hell. Why you? I mean, why would they want to attack a helpless old guy? Please forgive me for saying so, but you're just an old Japanese or Chinese guy. Why would they want you?"

"Chinese," the old man replied.

"What?" Dalton asked.

"You mentioned my nationality. I am of Chinese descent. However, for your information, I was born and raised in the United States, and as such, I am a US citizen. I am every bit as American as . . . well, as you are. But to answer your question, the Demons attacked me because they hate and fear me for the threat I pose to their demonic existence. You see, my new friend, I am a demon hunter and have been for the past forty or more years. I have spent a lifetime destroying demons."

Dalton was blown away by this revelation, "Demons, you say, real honest-to-goodness Hell-spawned demons? You're telling me that YOU hunt THEM? It looked to me like THEY were hunting YOU."

The old man nodded and replied, "Yes, you are correct. Last night, they were the hunters, and I was the one being hunted. That happens a lot. And by the way, now those horrible creatures will be hunting you."

"Me? What are you suggesting? Why would they want to hunt me? I just stumbled into that mess. All I did was try to help you."

"Yes, exactly. And that single act of kindness and the skills you used to help me told them you were a natural-born demon hunter, whether you were aware of that or not. Now, they have identified your soul and marked you as a threat. They will come for you as they came for me."

The old man reached his left hand and gently touched the puckered flesh on Dalton's face. Dalton flinched at his touch. "This is their mark. It will heal but will leave a scar. More importantly, it will leave a spiritual scar and will be a way for Hell's minions to find you. By helping me, you have unknowingly put yourself in Hell's crosshairs."

Dalton replied with frustration, "I guess no good deed truly does go unpunished. Wonderful, just friggin' wonderful!"

"Perhaps that's true. But there is something you need to remember, something you likely don't even know about yourself. The fact is, you have God-given skills and abilities to destroy these demons. If I may speak candidly, I have never met anyone with such strong capabilities in all my life. What you did with no prior knowledge or experience was phenomenal. With proper training, you could be one of the greatest demon hunters that ever lived."

"What? Don't be ridiculous. I'm no demon hunter. I'm . . . I mean . . . I'm nothing . . . a . . . a . . ."

"A lost soul. Yes, I can see that. Over the years, I have learned to distinguish between what is genuine and what is false. You are good and true. Your soul is pure, and your inner strength is beyond compare. That is why when you took my sacred Katana blades in your hands, you were able to perform so admirably. I'm sure you must have felt their power when you held them."

"Um . . . well, yes, I did feel something, a type of strength flowing through my body. It was unlike anything I had ever felt before."

The old Chinese man smiled, nodded, and said, "Yes, just as I suspected. Not everyone would feel that. In fact, if the blades had not sensed your worthiness, they would have never allowed you to pick them up. You have an incredible future ahead of you, my young warrior. You simply have to accept your fate. However, I can also sense that you have suffered a great loss, perhaps the loss of someone dear to you. This is why you are living here among the refuse of humanity, perhaps running away from life or hoping to find new meaning in your life. You are looking for answers where there are none. You constantly wonder why you are still alive when your loved one is gone. Am I right?"

"Um . . . Yes. Yes, I suppose you could say that."

"Was it a woman? Perhaps your wife? Was she the loss you suffered?"

"Yes," Dalton replied with a choked whisper, "My beautiful wife, Audrey, was taken from me way too soon."

"And you are alone in the world now?"

"Yes, I am."

"You feel like you are just passing the time, waiting for the day you can be with your wife again."

"Yes."

"Well, unfortunately, I wish I could tell you things will get better, that time will heal your wounds, and that someday you will love again. However, I can see the bond that joined your soul with your wife was so strong that even death could not break it. Things will not be all right, at least not for a very long time. It is possible that you will join your precious Audrey in the next life, but not, I believe, if you waste this life wallowing in sorrow. Your life now has a purpose; the forces of good have seen to that, my friend."

"Wow, aren't you just a bubbling font of good news and positive reinforcement this morning? First, you tell me Hell has marked me for life and wants to kill me and steal my soul. And now you tell me that unless I follow the road the universe has just laid out for me, I'm doomed to grieve for the rest of my miserable life. Then you tell me if I want to be with my Audrey again someday, my only choice is to become some comic book superhero demon hunter. Do you have any other useful tidbits of knowledge you might have forgotten to tell me about?"

"Actually, yes, I do. However, before we go there, may I ask your name? After all, I should know the name of the man who saved my life, shouldn't I?"

"My name is Hathaway Everett Dalton, but my friends just call me Doc."

"But you are not a doctor, are you? If you don't mind me asking."

"That's ok; I get asked that question a lot. No, I'm not a doctor. And to be honest, I've been called 'Doc' for as long as I can remember, yet I have no idea why. Even my Mamma called me Doc. And I think since you have condemned me to a future revolving around fighting demons and trying to stay on this side of the dirt, perhaps you might tell me your name?"

"That sounds fair to me. My name is Paul Chang. However, everyone calls me Mr. Chang."

"And which would you prefer I call you, Paul, Mr. Chang, or just Chang?"

The old man smiled and said, "You can call me Sensei . . . it means teacher."

"Of course, it does. Anyone who's ever seen The Karate Kid knows that. But why would I call you Sensei? Are you supposed to be my teacher or something? Wax on, wax off, and all that other Hollywood ninja crap?"

Chang shook his head slowly in disappointment and said, "Ah, so sad. Like most people, you disrespect what you do not understand. I should warn you that you will not survive long with that attitude."

Dalton was getting angry, "Yeah? Well, maybe surviving isn't high on my priority list. Maybe it would be better if I didn't. Then I could go and be with my wife. That sounds like a much better option to me right about now, anyway."

Chang remained frustratingly calm as he spoke, "If you dropped dead right now, that might be true, but you will never see your beloved wife again if one of those creatures finds you and kills you. These monsters will take your soul into the stinking pits of Hell, where you will suffer untold tortures and pain for eternity. I'm trying to explain to you that you have been marked. The life you had, no matter how miserable it might have been, is over. You no longer have a choice. You must either learn to fight and destroy these demons, or they will hunt you down and take possession of your soul."

Dalton reluctantly concluded that this strange old man was right. He wished now that he hadn't gone into that alley. He wished he hadn't fought off those creatures. However, as his father had always been fond of saying, "Wish in one hand and crap in the other and see which gets filled first."

Those demons in the alley had branded him. Dalton was marked, and he realized if he was going to survive, he would have to learn all he could from this old-timer as quickly as possible. This old guy looked like he had one foot in the grave and the other on a banana peel.

"Ok, Chang. You win. I suppose I have no choice. I'll train with you. When do we start?"

"We will start today, immediately. But not here. You will come to my home where I will give you a place to stay. I will feed you and teach you. You must promise to work hard, train hard, and learn everything you can. I am not young. My time is short, and you have so very much to learn."

Dalton said, "Then, in that case, we'd better get this show on the road."

CHAPTER 5

As he lay beneath the covers in his underwear, Dalton felt safe and comfortable as always when he was home. This place was much more than simply an apartment turned condo; it was his home. Dalton always felt it was akin to Superman's fortress of solitude, and rightfully so. It was his safe haven where no one or nothing could ever harm him.

It was protected from the entrance on the first floor to the deepest part of the basement to the highest point on the rooftop. There were other condo owners in the complex, yet not one was aware of the cloak of protection surrounding them. Each resident seemed to feel a unique warmth and security when they entered the building, but they all assumed it was nothing more than the comfort of returning home after a busy day. Little did they know that the strange, tall man dressed in black was the building's owner. They assumed he was a mysterious stranger who bought a condo just like they did. Nor did they know he had been the one who had "decorated" the common areas of the building in its strange and unique style.

The tenants saw the symbols etched into the glass front door and the intricate mosaic tile work on the floors and ceilings. However, to the casual onlooker, it was simply artwork. After all, similar etchings, paintings, and sculptures could be found all around the building. It was part of the building's decor, its personality, or so they presumed.

However, Dalton knew the images to be so much more. The symbols made the building invisible to even the most sophisticated of demons. As far as Hell was concerned, the building didn't exist. If a demonic creature did manage to stumble onto the building by some accident, touching any part of the place would result in the thing's immediate destruction. Yes, this building was Dalton's safe sanctuary from the horrors of the underworld and the monsters of the damned.

As he lay in bed, exhausted but not yet asleep, Dalton thought again about the man who had taught him so much and wondered why he was thinking about him now. It had been years since he had felt so intently about the strange Chinese man he had known first as Sensei, then as a friend, and who he eventually thought of as a father. Chang was also the man who had left Dalton a fortune, enabling him to take over the building from Chang and maintain its secrets as he had done all these years.

Chang had taught Dalton well. He gave Dalton the silver skull amulet with its intricately etched glyphs and glowing ruby eyes. Chang had also shown Dalton how to forge his own special swords and adorn them with a series of etchings needed when battling the forces of Hell. Each symbol possessed its unique, extraordinary power. Some of the etchings were to ward off evil, some to provide early warning, some to protect the sword from harm, and some to weaken the demonic forces, making them easier to defeat in battle. Many of the demons Dalton faced could regenerate severed body parts if given sufficient time, so weakening and destroying the monsters was paramount.

Lying in bed, staring at the ceiling, Dalton recalled how he had been confused by the skull medallion Chang originally wore on a chain around his neck. He had asked his teacher, "If we are supposed to be the good guys here to hunt down and destroy demons, why do you wear a skull with red jeweled eyes? Doesn't that seem like an evil symbol? I mean, shouldn't you have an angel or crucifix instead? Why the skull?"

Chang had explained to him, "This skull is the mirror image of its evil counterpart and therefore represents the opposite of that amulet in every way."

"Counterpart? I don't understand."

"You see, there is a thing, a most evil thing, that has existed since the dawn of time. It has taken many forms, as has been required throughout history, to succeed with whatever evil deed it needs to accomplish. It was once the tip of a staff owned by an evil queen in ancient Egypt. It once became an inset to a gunslinger's pearl handle pistols. It has even taken the form of a cell phone in recent years. But no matter its form, this artifact always appears as a skull with ruby eyes."

Dalton asked, "Can our amulet change its form as well?"

"No, it cannot. This talisman will always keep its current skull shape. It does not have that ability."

"What does the evil skull pendant do?" Dalton asked.

"It's a tool, a spell used by its master to open a direct portal to Hell. It can create a gateway by which demonic creatures can leave Hell and enter our world. The amulet I gave you exists to fight that evil whenever possible. It is the antithesis of the other, the evil one. This is why our amulet has the etchings while its counterpart is smooth."

Dalton looked shocked as he stared at the shining silver skull, "Are you saying that skull you wear is as old as its evil twin? Because it looks brand new."

"No, it is not quite that old. However, it is thousands of years old, having been hand-forged eons ago by our predecessors who sought to fight the evil brought to earth by the skull amulet. It looks new because it always will look new, as its evil counterpart will always look new. One is protected by good, while evil forces protect the other. Yet both are ancient."

"Do you know where the other amulet is now, the evil one?"

"I do not know for certain," Chang replied, "The last I heard about it, the evil skull was in the possession of a business executive known as R. John Showalter, but that was more than a decade ago. It could be anywhere in the world by now. It changes hands as Hell requires."

"Can it be destroyed? Can our amulet destroy it?"

Chang hesitated, then said, "I don't know, and I hope I never find out. The truth is, I fear what might happen if our medallion came in contact with the evil one."

"You think it might destroy ours?"

"I fear they might destroy each other and possibly anyone near them."

Dalton said, "Ok. That's a valuable lesson for me to remember. We've seen demons trying to enter our world through those cracks in the ground. Is that the result of that other skull amulet thing?"

Chang said, "I don't know for sure, but I suppose it could be possible. However, in order for it to be used against us, the current master would have to target us specifically, and I don't believe that's what is happening. Although the artifact does open portals, it is generally done by the earthbound Demon that processes it. It can open a crack in the earth or a portal in the very air around you. I believe we have been experiencing portals opened by other demons specifically sent to kill us. They are similar to those appearing from portals opened by the amulet, but the two situations may not be connected. I have no way of knowing this for certain since all that is available to me is supposition."

Dalton questioned, "You said 'earthbound demons'; does that mean what I think it means?"

"Yes, unfortunately, it does. One of the things I have not yet shared with you is the fact that demons walk among us. They disguise themselves as humans and do so quite cleverly. However, they are not human. The last known owner of the evil amulet, R. John Showalter, is one such earthbound demon. They are a higher form of demon than those we have fought in the past. Those creatures who come up to battle are perhaps the lowest forms of demons. They are essentially cannon fodder, sent to kill us, even though they have little chance of doing so, thanks to our skills. They can, however, get in the occasional lucky shot if we are not careful enough. I suppose it's Hell's version of throwing a handful of darts blindfolded, hoping one might hit the bullseye."

"So, let me get this straight. Are you saying actual higher-level demons exist today on Earth, and we can't locate them or do anything to stop them?"

"We can detect them, and there are things we can do to stop them. However, locating them is difficult, and what's much worse is that it's even more difficult to destroy them. Remember that these creatures live among us, appearing to be normal humans. They have human friends, and many of those associates are in high places. Most are unaware of their origins, but others may be fellow demons. Some of these demons appear as normal, typical suburban men or women. Some even have families. Of course, the entire family image is a sham established to camouflage a group of demons. However, to their friends and neighbors, they appear as normal as you and I do."

"But if we know what they are, don't we have a responsibility to destroy them?" Dalton asked.

"Perhaps we do. Perhaps not. Unfortunately, there is no guidebook for demon hunters with a list of responsibilities and a collection of dos and don'ts. We are essentially writing the rule book as we go along. But imagine, for a moment, trying to assassinate the governor of any state. It would be challenging for you not to get caught or killed. Even though you might know he is a demon, no one else does. As a result, they would all see you as a psychopath, a madman who killed their beloved governor. Do you understand what I'm trying to tell you?"

"You're saying there are demons you know about but cannot touch."

"Not cannot, but perhaps 'should not' is a better explanation. You see, it can be very difficult. Identifying them is hard enough. Destroying them is even harder."

Dalton asked, "Will you teach me to identify them?"

"I will. It will be part of your training. But you must understand something, which is probably the hardest aspect of demon hunting for you to accept. Just as a doctor cannot save all of his patients, you will not be able to destroy all of the earthbound demons you learn about. You will have to come to terms with that and pick those battles you can win, or this journey you are taking will be a short one. Do you understand what I'm trying to tell you?"

"Yes, I believe I do. I cannot risk the continued success of my demon-hunting responsibilities for the sake of one demon, who I might not be able to get to successfully. I assume you know of some of these?"

"I know of many, unfortunately, and I'm sure there are many I don't know about either. I can't begin to tell you how it pains me to see them walking about causing chaos in our world while their followers mindlessly do their bidding. Think for a moment about a celebrity who takes a stand against something you find pure and sacred. Say, for example, any of the symbols of our country, such as our flag. The demon, posing as a human, may have hundreds or thousands of followers and, through his charismatic personality, can convince them that these sacred symbols represent evil. Then, before you know it, those disciples are burning our flag in protest, destroying historical monuments, perhaps rioting, and they have no idea that a demon is orchestrating everything they are doing."

This particular aspect of his new life disturbed Dalton, as his Sensei knew it would. The idea of demons from Hell occupying positions of power in his country was something he had trouble accepting. He always felt people like certain politicians and corporate CEOs were heartless sociopaths who pretended to care about their underlings but, in reality, cared about no one but themselves. However, the idea that any of them might actually be demons called up from Hell to cause chaos among humanity was hard to wrap his head around at first.

Then, Dalton recalled companies he had worked for and how they treated their employees. Suddenly, the idea didn't seem quite so out of the ordinary. He had worked for corporations that had been so poorly managed that he would often wonder if the managers were trying to destroy the company rather than helping it succeed. Other companies seemed to be run by tyrants who treated their workers like slaves.

He realized the very idea of a corporation itself seemed like a concept originating in the depths of Hell. After all, a corporation was, by definition, a non-entity. It was implemented to protect its management from legal action from outsiders. So, in essence, employees of a corporation work for and are paid by an entity that does not physically exist. Even the top-level management and board of directors are employees of the same non-existent being. The more Dalton thought about it, the more it made sense.

Dalton said, "You know, Sensei, I believe you're right about that. I suspect there are a lot of demons in high places."

"There are. And most of those demons are so firmly entrenched in their positions of power that they can't be touched. They are only removed when another, more powerful demon takes their place. Then, they are moved to another position. Did you ever hear a coworker say, 'I have no idea how that guy holds onto his job'? Or maybe you heard an expression like 'these big wigs always take care of their own'? I'm sure you must have."

"Yes, I have heard that many times. More importantly, I have seen it firsthand as well."

"Chances are pretty good; in those situations, the big man at the company and several, if not all, of his top-tier management team members were either demons or human servants of demons."

"Human servants? You mean regular human beings who knowingly serve these creatures?"

"Yes, that's exactly what I mean. These people have sold their souls to these demons with the hopes of having a better place in the hierarchy of Hell someday when they cross over. But they are fools, as they will likely end up being tortured endlessly before being sent to challenge us and be destroyed. This is how the great deceiver operates."

Dalton began to wonder, since there were so many demons hiding behind masks of humanity, if there must also be more demon hunters out there doing their best to rid the world of those monsters.

He inquired, "Tell me, Sensei, are there others like you and me out there? You know, demon hunters?"

"I don't know. There might be. I would think there would have to be, but I have never encountered any. I was trained by a man who came before me as I am training you. My master has passed on, and I will likewise cross over someday. You will spend the rest of your life destroying demons when you have completed your training. That is all I know for sure."

After a while, as his eyes became heavy, Dalton's memories of his teacher began to muddle and blend in with other memories as he passed from the waking world into sleep and to the realm of dreams.

CHAPTER 6

Dalton opened his eyes and found he was alone in an alley, the same alley where he had defeated the Demon earlier that evening. However, things were different now. The flaming crack in the earth had returned, as did the snake-like creatures he had destroyed. He remembered that final snake creature saying his beloved wife was with them in Hell. But he knew that had to be impossible.

As he had told the serpent who tried to goad him, his wife had been a living angel, and there was no way she would have ended up anywhere close to Hell.

"But how can you be sure?" From a dark corner to his right, a voice said, "How can you pretend to be so confident when you really don't know."

Dalton knew that voice. How could he help but know it? After all, he had trained with the man day in and day out for three solid years. But it couldn't be his Sensei. Paul Chang had been dead for almost seven years. Yet Dalton knew his teacher's voice as well as his own.

He turned and stared into the dark shadows, still present despite the light from the fiery crack in the earth behind him. Dalton heard a scraping noise like metal being dragged across the blacktop. Dalton saw a diminutive figure lurching and twitching its way into the light as he looked on. He couldn't believe his eyes.

The figure was Chang, his Sensei, but the pitiful creature shambling before him scarcely resembled his former teacher. He was barely more than skin hanging on bones, practically naked save for tattered remnants of a filthy yellowed fabric serving as a rudimentary loin cloth. His flesh was gray and mottled, covered in open, festering sores. Thin, rusted wires pierced the flesh of his face, connecting to his wrists and ankles, making him look like a human marionette but one in unimaginable pain. The Chang thing lumbered toward Dalton with its right hand outstretched.

Through a dangling, half-functioning lower jaw, the horrid creature said, "Come with us, Dalton. Hell's not such a bad place. I love it there. Come with me; Audrey is in Hell waiting for you. She misses you and is suffering more than you could ever comprehend, and it's all your fault. Hell hates you for what you have done to its minions as they hated me. The demons have your wife's soul. I can assure you the pain they are inflicting on her is a thousand times worse than her cancer pain ever was. It's all because of you; it's all your fault.

"But you can make Audrey's pain stop, Dalton. You can make things right. If you'd only give up and let them have your soul, they would leave Audrey alone. If not, the agony will continue for eternity. And you know sooner or later, they'll get you anyway. They got my soul, Dalton, and I was your mentor and one of the best. If they managed to get me, what chance can you hope to have? I was a master demon hunter long before you knew such things existed. I spent most of my life fighting for the light, struggling to keep the forces of darkness at bay. But they got me anyway, Dalton, as they'll get you. Make things easy on yourself or, more importantly, make things easier on your beloved wife. Audrey doesn't deserve to suffer for your crimes."

Dalton screamed at the walking skeleton, "You lie. That's what you servants of Hell always do. You lie to convince me to do what you want, but I won't fall for it. You aren't my Sensei. My Sensei isn't in Hell, and neither is Audrey."

"Don't be so sure, Doc, my darling," a faint voice called from behind him.

Dalton turned at the sound of the voice he hadn't heard in over a decade, a voice he knew and would always love. It was the voice of his loving wife, Audrey. He couldn't believe his eyes; he was looking at Audrey as she had appeared before cancer had ravaged her. She was healthy and beautiful with pink skin and bright, lovely eyes. She wore a sheer translucent yellow and white gown. It was very low-cut, exposing her gorgeous, round cleavage, reminding Dalton of how long it had been since he had been with her. Audrey's smile was radiant, the same smile he had fallen in love with so many years earlier.

"A . . . Au . . . Audrey? Is that really you?" He asked, knowing it couldn't possibly be her but wanting to believe it was, needing to believe.

"Of course, it's me, my love. I've come to take you home, be by my side again, and be with me forever."

Dalton said, "If only that were true. If only that could be true. I would give anything to be with you again, Audrey."

"Anything?" Audrey asked. But her voice had changed somewhat, sounding less like his late wife's voice and more like a deeper alto voice, becoming a low guttural growl. Dalton sensed something was wrong. "Anything, my darling? Would you give your immortal soul?"

Then Audrey began to change. Her healthy glow disappeared as her skin became a dusky gray. Dozens of pus-oozing sores appeared on her arms, legs, face, and chest. Dalton could see her once beautiful breasts withering to empty sacks of sagging skin before his eyes through her translucent dressing gown. Maggots bored in and out of her weeping sores, and insects flew about her, landing on her mottled flesh long enough to lay eggs in her festering wounds.

Her face had become that of an ancient, hideous old crone. As the hag opened her mouth to speak, a few rotting tombstone teeth dropped to the paving with a tiny clinking sound. Her once beautiful long blonde hair was white as snow and had fallen out in clumps, flying away on the breeze, leaving bare patches of the putrefying scalp in their wake.

The Audrey creature stepped toward Dalton, reaching her bony arms and extending her gnarled fingers. Her shriveled lips began to move, and Dalton heard her hissing in a snake-like voice, "Come with me, baby. I love you. Kisssss me, my darling."

Dalton took a step backward as the horrid creature opened its mouth wider as if to shout, and a flood of maggots regurgitated from her broken maw and poured over her lips like a waterfall of vermin. Dalton couldn't stand it anymore and screamed, "Nooooooooo!"

CHAPTER 7

Dalton sat up in bed with a start, his heart pounding like a drummer on speed and his eyes wide as saucers. Cold sweat streamed from every pore in his body, soaking his underwear and even his bedsheets. A sour stench surrounded him as he realized he would have to take yet another shower, not to mention that he'd have to change and wash all his bedding.

He threw his legs over the side of the bed and sat for several minutes, panting like a dog, waiting for his heart to slow to some semblance of normalcy. The cool floor felt reassuring on his bare feet. Already, the sleep was rapidly leaving him and taking away the memories of his nightmare. He assumed the dream was some derivative of several earlier bad dreams he had remembered involving Sensei Chang and his wife, Audrey. Only nightmares like those could awaken him with such ferocity.

Those dreams always seemed ridiculous in the light of day, but they were so real and terrifying in the world of sleep. Dalton looked at the digital clock on his end table and saw it was 1:11 a.m. He knew he couldn't get back to sleep for quite a while, if at all. Although this always happened to him after a nightmare, he found it unusual under the current circumstances. Dalton recalled how usually, after a battle like the one he had tonight, he would collapse with exhaustion as he had done, but typically, he wouldn't wake up for many hours. Yet here he was, wide awake.

As he stared into the darkness of his bedroom, Dalton felt a rumbling in his stomach and realized he couldn't recall the last time he had eaten. He hadn't been to his usual breakfast spot that morning, so it was entirely possible that he hadn't eaten since the previous day. Maybe a trip to Max's around the corner for a late-night snack might be what Dalton needed to help him relax. God knew it wouldn't do him any good if he chose to walk around, staring at his sparsely decorated apartment. Maybe he'd also pick up a book or a magazine at Max's. Reading often helped his mind relax enough for him to fall asleep.

Max's store always had a good selection of snacks and pre-made cold sandwiches. Dalton figured he might feel considerably better if he picked up a few subs, maybe a bag of chips and an ice-cold soda. So, after freshening up and changing, it looked like he would go off to Max's.

CHAPTER 8

Dalton opened the front door and walked through the entrance into Max's 24-7 convenience store. As he crossed the threshold, he heard the familiar yet annoying sound of the electronic warning buzzer announcing his arrival.

"Good Lord, that's a godawful sound!" Dalton thought. Considering his calling in life, Dalton had heard more than his share of horrible sounds; the howls of the possessed, the screams of the tournament damned, the bellows of demons. He had experienced noises most humans could scarcely imagine, sounds that were likely to drive lesser men insane. Yet none of those sounds tormented him like that infernal buzzer did each time he walked through the door.

If it weren't because he cared greatly for this store and its owner, Dalton would have driven his blade through the guts of the tormenting buzzer long ago. But now, he wouldn't do that. For Dalton, this place had become an oasis in the filthy wasteland of the miserable city. That was why he wasn't in the least bit concerned about appearing conspicuous with his long black leather coat, hat, boots, and, of course, his hidden weaponry. Max and all of his employees knew and respected Dalton. Although they didn't know what Dalton did for a living, they knew he never left his home without weapons; it was just part of how he lived his life.

The Max in Max's was Maximillian Padu, an Indian immigrant who had opened his first convenience store thirty years earlier and now had a small chain of more than a dozen. Dalton frequented this store as it was only a few blocks from his apartment. Max's employees were always glad when Dalton stopped by. They all understood Dalton was a blessing to have as a friend and a curse to have as an enemy.

His huge presence and menacing appearance were excellent deterrents for potential criminals whenever he was in the store. No one in their right mind would dare to rob a place if they knew Doc Dalton was in the house. As Dalton entered the store, he saw that Carlos DeJesus was behind the counter. Carlos was known on the street as C.J., the DJ, because of his side business, which involved playing tunes for various events throughout the neighborhood.

Dalton nodded at the young man as he passed the counter, offering a perfunctory greeting, "C.J."

"Doc," C.J. replied with equal brevity.

"All good?"

"Yep. All good, slow night."

"Good. Quiet is good."

"And you?" C.J. inquired.

"Way too busy."

"No rest for the weary."

"True that," Dalton replied.

Dalton made his way down the long aisle to the back of the store, where they kept the self-service soft drink machines. He'd be getting the same thing he always got: a 44-ounce cup of ice filled three-quarters of the way with Diet Coke and the last quarter with original Coke to help take some of the bite out of the diet drink.

Although this place was only a minimart, it followed the same philosophies as large supermarkets. All the essentials, such as milk, bread, eggs, toilet paper, and the like, were kept at the rear of the store. This way, customers had to walk past and hopefully buy the less-needed items that caught their attention. The same was true for self-serve things like soda, ice cream, and the ever-popular slushy machines. The only exceptions were tobacco products like cigarettes, cigars, chew, snuff, and even vaping supplies. Those could always be found behind the counter in the front end of the store. He supposed that was because of some government regulation or other. Even the beer and wine were located toward the back of the place.

"Smart marketing," Dalton thought as he did every time he walked back to get his drink. As he made his way up the aisle, he noticed some soup cans on the rack not far from the soda dispensers. He stopped briefly, focusing on a small can of tomato soup. There seemed to be nothing special about the can at first, but then something happened. Dalton might have been troubled if it had been the first time such a thing had occurred. But things like this often happened to him, and he had learned to pay attention when they did.

The rest of the soup cans on the shelves seemed to lose their color and sharpness, fading into a dark black-and-white background. In contrast, the colors on the red and white label of the tomato soup can became increasingly vibrant, glowing with effervescence. Dalton reached down and picked the can from the shelf. He was suddenly reminded of his childhood and how his mother would make him grilled cheese sandwiches and tomato soup.

Young Hathaway Dalton, or Little Doc, as his mother called him when he was a child, loved the soup and sandwich combination and looked forward to it whenever his mother made it. He had never considered making it for himself, but maybe he would tonight. He had cheese and bread at home; he needed the soup. Dalton took the can with him, determined to have a delicious nostalgic snack this evening, followed by the remainder of his good night's sleep.

As he turned the corner and began filling a cup with his favorite Diet Coke/Coke mixture, he heard the annoying buzzer go off at the front of the store as the door was opened. He felt the hairs on the back of his neck stand on end. The amulet on his chest began to vibrate lightly. Dalton knew a threat was coming, but one of the human variety. Then, a few seconds later, he heard a voice shouting at the front of the store.

"Put your hands where we can see them, scum-sucker, and open that cash register. No funny stuff, or we'll splatter your brains all over the cigarette case."

"A robbery. Probably a couple of crackheads," Dalton thought as his fantasy of grilled cheese and tomato soup began to dissolve, evaporating into the harshness of reality. His thoughts were quickly replaced by anger, frustration, and general disappointment with his fellow man. Dalton had no patience for junkies, with their jittery, twitching arms and lunatic flitting eyes. They were as bothersome as the demons he regularly hunted, maybe more so since they were still human, although barely human. Dalton knew this kind of situation could spiral out of control very quickly.

He held his soda in his left hand and his soup can in his right as he walked slowly and deliberately back down the aisle toward the front of the store. He did so out in the open without attempting to hide or sneak up on the two punks turned would-be robbers. Often, just seeing Dalton and his intimidating appearance was enough to scare off characters like those. However, it was instantly obvious that the pair were too hyped up on whatever they had snorted, swallowed, or shot into their veins to have any fear. They were both pointing, shaking guns at C.J., who stood calmly with his hands still under the counter.

Dalton understood better than these two idiots did that if and when they screwed up, they would be stepping off this mortal coil and would quickly find their way through the fiery gates of Hell this night. Go to Hell, go directly to Hell, do not pass GO, and do not collect $200. With peripheral vision, C.J. saw

Dalton coming down the aisle and relaxed a bit, ready to make his move when the right moment came.

Dalton shouted, "Hey, what the Hell do you two numb-nuts think you're doing?"

What happened next took place from beginning to end, over about five seconds, but it seemed to play out in slow motion like a scene from a particularly violent Sam Peckinpah movie. After almost dropping his gun, the first robber turned and pointed it directly at Dalton. Dalton hoped he wouldn't be stupid enough to try to shoot him, but he suddenly realized the idiot was about to make his play.

However, before the junkie's twitching fingers could pull the trigger, Dalton hurled the tomato soup can with an unimaginable speed, so fast that no eyes save Dalton's own could hope to follow it. Within a millisecond, the soup can smashed against the robber's forehead, splitting his skull open down the center and forcing his brain matter to explode out backward, showering his screaming partner with gore.

One second later, C.J. came up from under the counter with a double-barrel sawed-off shotgun. The blast from the weapon was deafening in the small confines of the store. However, the noise didn't matter to the second thug, as his head was no longer attached to his body. It was nowhere to be seen unless you counted the splatter of blood, flesh, bone, teeth, and gray matter decorating the shelves along the wall behind him.

Then, a moment later, the store was as silent as a tomb. The smell of gunfire hung in the air, as did the stench of the junkies' blood and involuntarily released bowels and bladders.

"Sorry about the noise," C.J. said to Dalton without taking his eyes from the carnage on the floor below.

"Sorry about the mess," Dalton said, still staring at the two corpses.

"No problem, we got people," C.J. replied as he picked up his cell phone and speed-dialed a number.

"Cops?" Dalton asked, knowing the answer before C.J. even spoke.

"Yeah, right," he said with a laugh. There would be no police called to this scene.

"Oh, right, people. It's good to have people," Dalton said matter-of-factly.

C.J. replied, "Damn straight."

Dalton got the gist of what was going down from C.J.'s half of the conversation when the call was eventually answered.

"Yo, Chino . . . Yeah, this is C.J. We need some . . . house-keeping . . . Yeah, again . . . I know . . . it's the neighborhood, right? Do me a favor and send Johnny and his crew . . . Yeah, it's really messy . . . Same deal? Cash, that's right. Ok, thanks." He disconnected the call.

"Housekeeping?" Dalton said with a grin.

"Yeah, housekeeping," C.J. replied.

"Friends?"

"In a matter of speaking."

"It's good to have friends," Dalton said.

"Yep, it certainly is," C.J. agreed.

Dalton looked around the store and asked, "Security cameras?"

"Fakes."

Dalton nodded with understanding.

C.J. looked uncomfortable, then said, "Look, Doc, not to be rude or sound ungrateful, but it would probably be best if you weren't here when the crew gets here. They prefer to work, shall we say, without an audience, if you get my drift."

"Sure, no problem."

Dalton lifted his cup of soda, which he still held in his left hand, and said, "I owe you for the soda . . . and the soup can."

C.J. laughed, "No sweat. The drink is on the house, my friend. If you want to, you can grab another can. That one's sort of . . . you know, dented."

The can was still embedded deep in the dead man's skull, sitting among the remnants of his no longer functioning brain.

"Thanks, but I think I'll pass. I'm suddenly not in the mood for tomato soup."

C.J. looked down at the pool of blood spreading across the vinyl floor and said, "Yeah, I s'pose not."

Dalton stepped over the two corpses and grabbed the door handle.

"Hey, Doc, can you do me a solid and turn that sign on the door around to 'closed'?" C.J. asked as he began flipping switches and turning off most of the lights in the store.

"Sure, no problem. See you later?" Doc asked.

"Yeah, most likely. See ya when I see ya."

Dalton opened the door to leave, heard the annoying entry buzzer, looked up at it, and thought, "One of these days . . ."

CHAPTER 9

Dalton started walking back to his apartment, and as he turned the corner and glanced back at the store, he saw a dark black windowless van pulling up outside of Max's. Three large men in dark coveralls, wearing black gloves and matching surgical masks, got out and went to the back of the vehicle. They opened the back and took buckets, mops, and heavy plastic trash bags. Then they walked toward the front door, glancing up and down the street, ensuring they were alone.

C.J. came out and held the door to let them in. Two of the men followed C.J. inside, while one carrying a large handgun waited outside to discourage any unlikely onlookers. Dalton saw one of the men look up angrily as they passed the threshold. Apparently, the cleanup man didn't like the buzzer any more than Dalton did. He shook his head and chuckled to himself as he headed home.

Less than a block from his apartment, the silver skull medallion began to vibrate furiously against Dalton's chest. He looked down and saw the ruby-red eyes start to glow brightly. He knew what that meant. It was the same thing it always meant. But as he looked around, he didn't see the ground splitting open or flames shooting up as he would have expected. He saw nothing. Then he looked ahead and saw someone turning the corner. The figure was shadowed but was a nondescript man dressed somewhat like himself.

The man appeared as tall as Dalton and wore a dark Fedora-styled hat, a long black trench coat with dark pants and shoes beneath. At first glance, he seemed to be a businessman walking home from work. But it was the middle of the night. No businessman in his right mind walked these city streets at night. The man stopped as he rounded the corner and stood silently. Although the figure was a block away and his face could not be seen, Dalton felt the man's gaze staring at him, seeming to stare right through him.

Dalton wondered, "Who is this guy? What does he want? Is he the one causing all my demon warnings to go on high alert?"

That was when the man began to run toward Dalton. His trench coat flapped open as he did, and Dalton could see the glimmer of Katana blades, again very similar to his own. Dalton stood still, unsure of what was happening but preparing for a battle he knew was coming. As the stranger ran toward him, Dalton withdrew his own Katana blades.

As the attacker's sword came striking down, the blade in Dalton's right hand blocked the blow as the sound of metal against metal rang through the otherwise silent night. Sparks flew as the blades collided repeatedly. It was as if the stranger knew every move Dalton would make before he made it and parried his every thrust. Dalton had never experienced anything like this before.

"I feel like I'm fighting myself," he thought as he thrust his blade toward the stranger's throat, only to have it blocked by the man's blade. "What manner of demon is this?"

Dalton was sure his attacker was not just some low-level demon but was likely one of the higher-level demons Chang had warned him about. That made sense because this creature came in human form without the fire and theatrics of the lesser demons. However, this would-be assassin had a superior skill set to any monster he had previously encountered. Dalton wished this attack had come on the heels of a restful night's sleep but knew he had no choice but to make do and hope his skills would rise to the challenge.

He blocked two more of the stranger's attacks and had his next three attempts to kill the demon blocked in kind. Dalton backed away a few feet to devise an alternate plan when, to his surprise, the stranger did the same.

"Who or what in Hell are you?" Dalton asked.

The stranger remained silent, standing with his swords down by his sides. There was something oddly familiar about how the man stood and held himself and his swords. Then, it suddenly all began to make sense: how the stranger could match him blow by blow. Yet such a thing was impossible! That is to say, Dalton believed it was impossible. Now he understood everything. This creature, this demon, was an alternate version of himself.

He saw the demon raise its head slightly in recognition as if it had heard Dalton's innermost thoughts and somehow knew Dalton had realized the creature's nature. Then, the man took off his Fedora and tossed it into the street. Dalton could see the demon's face in the light from a nearby streetlight. It was his face, yet not entirely. It was as if the creature's face was trying to form on a canvas of flesh but had only partially completed the transformation. It reminded Dalton of a picture taken slightly out of focus. However, it was close enough for Dalton to see the slowly forming resemblance.

Dalton hoped that because the creature appeared to be an incomplete representation of himself, its intelligence was perhaps as vague as its face. But then Dalton realized that was a false hope since the demon had already proven he could fight with all the skill Dalton had, the same talent that had helped Dalton survive all these years. How was that possible? What could he do? How could he beat a creature who knew his moves and could anticipate what he would do next?

Then, an understanding hit him. This creature, this demon, used skills Dalton had exhibited in battling other minions of

Hell. He always wondered why Hell had sent such low-level demons to fight him. He understood now. These monsters were sent to fight him so those in Hell could watch and study him to learn his movements and strategies. They wanted to create a copy of Dalton, who was skilled and knowledgeable in all his fighting techniques. The creature standing down the street from him resulted from those studies. Dalton feared it might be all over for him when the demon attacked again. Unless . . .

That was it! He realized he had to up his game. He couldn't rely on his past fighting techniques. He had to do something unorthodox, something completely off the wall and out of character. What that might be, he didn't know yet, but what he did know was the only way to beat himself was not to be able to anticipate what he might do.

The demon lifted his swords again as he began to charge toward Dalton, something Dalton himself had done to other monsters many times before. Seeing this creature coming at him in such a manner was so strange. Typically, Dalton would counterattack, charge, and meet the attacker head-on. But not this time. Dalton stood with his hands tightly around the grips of his Katana blades, still unsure of his next move, which he determined was good. Because if he didn't know what he would do, then the demon couldn't know either.

As the monster reached him, just a millisecond before his swords would have relieved Dalton of his head, Dalton dropped to the ground and rolled toward the demon. Dalton's rolling body caught the creature completely off guard; its legs were knocked out from under it. As the devil fell face forward to the ground, Dalton stood behind the fallen monster and drove his blades down into the demon's back and straight through it.

The creature twitched and convulsed for several seconds before finally stopping its spastic gyrations and lying still. Then, the demon burst into flames within a few seconds and was rapidly consumed by the fire. Soon, all that remained was a pile of burnt ashes. A moment later, a strong wind came out of nowhere and blew the remains away. It also picked up the stranger's hat and carried it with the ashes.

"Ok then," Dalton said as he stared at the barely visible dust trail, which was all that remained of his Hell-spawned doppelganger.

He slowly replaced his Katana blades in their sheaths and stood listening to the silence that had returned to the night. He wondered if he was correct about what had just happened. Had Hell sent this demonic replication of himself to kill him, or was its purpose to study him further, to learn more about his fighting techniques? Most likely, it had served both purposes. If so, that would mean the next time they sent a clone of him, this new version would be harder to beat than this one. And where would it end?

Sensei Chang had never warned him about such trickery. Perhaps it had never been tried against his teacher. Whatever the case, he would deal with this problem and any other demon clones Hell sent his way when the time came. But for now, the danger was past, and he could return to the safety of his condo and finish his night's sleep. He was exhausted enough to do just that.

CHAPTER 10

The morning light shone through the tall bedroom windows as Dalton squinted through sleepy eyes at the clock on his nightstand.

He mumbled, "Nine . . . forty . . . eight . . . wait a minute! Nine forty-eight? I never sleep this late. I can't remember the last time I slept so late."

Then again, neither could he recall the last time he had battled demons, killed armed robbers, and fought a demonic version of himself, all within the same twenty-four-hour period—no wonder he had been so tired.

He climbed out of bed, realizing that he ached from head to toe as soon as his feet hit the floor. He shuffled like a man twice his age into the bathroom for his morning ritual. He stood under a hot shower for the second time in less than twelve hours. Yes, he needed to be cleaned, but more than that, the hot water felt incredible on his aching muscles, and the steam did wonders to open up his sinuses.

Although Dalton hated to admit it, he was getting older, and unlike most men his age, he had put a lot of wear and tear mileage on his biological odometer. Most professional athletes hung up their jockstraps years before they reached the age when Dalton first started hunting demons. Now, a decade later, he was tired. No, being tired would have been an improvement; he was exhausted. But what could he do?

He learned from Master Chang that the profession he had accidentally found himself thrust into was not precisely the sort of job you could walk away from and forget. When you've managed to piss off most of the demons in Hell and destroy countless others, you tend to find yourself the target of many demonic adverse opinions. When every demon in Hell knows your name, your reputation, and the value of the price the great deceiver himself has put on your soul, you don't exactly get to disappear into a villa along a secluded beach in the Caribbean.

No way, Jose. Every time you set foot outside your apartment sanctuary, you become a target for snipers from Hell. Dalton realized he was in this game to the bitter end, or he'd have to become a recluse and never leave his building. How long would that last? How long would it be until the denizens of darkness figured out how to get around the complex collection of charms, spells, and talismans he had created to protect his sanctuary? As it was, he constantly monitored and refortified the building's many defenses. What would happen if he became too old or disabled to handle this responsibility? Would he sit in his apartment, waiting for demons to come up through the floorboards and drag his soul to Hell?

Then, he realized less than a decade earlier that his Sensei Chang had faced the same dilemma. Granted, Chang had been probably twenty years older than Dalton presently was, which explained the urgency of his need to train Dalton. But surely, Chang had to know he needed an apprentice to take his place eventually.

Once Chang felt Dalton was ready to go off on his own, the master laid down one day in his bed, closed his eyes, and peacefully passed on before Hell knew he was dying. By having Dalton around not only to protect him but to battle and distract the demons, Chang's soul could pass on peacefully, and by the time Hell realized it, well, it was simply too late.

Perhaps now might be the time for Dalton to consider look-ing for an apprentice to train. Then again, how could he even hope to do that? It wasn't the sort of profession people lined up to apply for. It wasn't the easiest sell, either. Dalton thought about a potential classified ad, such as, "Help wanted. Demon Hunter— looking for an apprentice to battle the forces of Hell. The money sucks, and Hell's minions will try to destroy you and steal your soul at every opportunity for the rest of your natural life."

"That ought to get 'em beating down the doors to get in," Dalton thought sarcastically. Had he not lost his beloved wife, he never would have gone into the spiral of depression, and he wouldn't have lived under a bridge among the homeless. Had he not tried to save that strange old man, who would later become his Sensei, Dalton never would have been marked for death by the demons from Hell.

That got Dalton thinking; maybe that fateful night he ran into the alley to save the poor old man might not have been as much of a happenstance as he had first thought. What if Chang hadn't been in as much trouble as Dalton had imagined? What if it all had been an audition?

He supposed that scenario might be plausible. After all, Chang was a sly old fox. You don't survive hunting demons for forty years without some tricks up your sleeve. Dalton knew that from experience. Chang had recruited him more than a decade ago, and now Master Chang was gone, and Doc Dalton, Demon Hunter, was alone.

"So much for me finding someone dumb enough to want to ruin his life and risk his immortal soul to hunt and destroy demons. And to what end?" Dalton thought. He knew the sup-ply of damned souls was a never-ending and always-growing commodity. He had been hunting demons for only a blip on the landscape of time, and his master had been before him for over 40 years. Yet new monsters have appeared daily in Hell since the dawn of time. His actions likely amounted to no more than those of a crazy man trying to empty the Atlantic Ocean with a spoon.

Then he realized what was happening to him. The same thing happened on other occasions when he was exhausted. He doubted his purpose. And who could blame him? He was running headfirst into a hurricane of evil. He was trying to swim against the force of a demonic Tsunami. He was one man alone against all the powers of Hell. Sure, it was a crappy job, but he supposed somebody had to do it. But why him? Because he was good at it, that's why. Dalton had to admit he was probably one of the best.

Dalton turned off the shower and stepped out to dry off. Once again, the healing effects of a hot shower had done their work. His muscles hardly ached any longer, and he was alert and ready to take on another day. More importantly, that fleeting feeling of melancholy that accosted him was rapidly fading. If fate decided he would find someone to be his protege, so be it. He decided he wouldn't concern himself with it any longer until then. Today was another day.

CHAPTER 11

Dalton sat quietly at the counter of his favorite breakfast place, just a few blocks away from his building. It was a local diner, usually busy with many satisfied customers. A huge plate of scrambled eggs, bacon, sausage, pancakes, and home fries appeared on the counter before him. The waitress who brought the food was a hot red-headed number named Agnes. She was built with more curves than the Mississippi River and more moves than a crate of Exlax. Dalton also knew that every wiggle she made was meant for him to see.

Dalton felt the familiar pang of guilt he always experienced when he caught himself gawking at women. It made him feel as if he was somehow diminishing the memory of his beloved late wife. She might have been years in the ground, but she was always with him in his heart.

When Audrey was alive, had she caught him noticing another woman, he would joke and say, "Just because I'm on a diet doesn't mean I can't check out the menu." She would smile and shake her head at the lame and stale joke. Audrey knew Dalton loved her more than life and would never be unfaithful. However, those days were gone forever. Audrey was gone forever, yet Dalton still could not allow himself to consider being with another woman. The wedding band he still wore had become a talisman, every bit as much as his skull amulet, probably more so.

Dalton's Katana blades, usually hanging by his sides, were now in a closet near the entrance to the diner. The owner always insisted Dalton store them there when he came to eat. Dalton didn't mind the slight inconvenience as he had plenty of other weapons hidden under his long coat for protection. The owner knew about those as well, but as far as he was concerned, if the patrons couldn't see them, he didn't care if Dalton kept a nuclear warhead in his coat. Out of sight, out of mind.

Taking his eyes off Agnes' posterior performance, Dalton stared into his cup of boiled water, watching the clear liquid turn brownish orange. A winding stream of tea crept from the teabag dangling over the side of the cup. He could smell its aroma in the rising clouds of steam. Dalton could have quickly sped things along by squeezing the teabag but chose not to. Something seemed to be relaxing, if not hypnotic, about watching this bag of tea leaves transform clear water into his favorite delicious hot drink.

He understood that most people might think him strange for feeling as Dalton did. Then again, most people didn't possess the same appreciation for the simpler things in life as he did. To say Dalton was nothing like most people was the understatement of understatements.

Dalton understood, of course, why he would never be like everyone else again. It was because of the nature of his job. That is, if one could consider what he did as a profession. When thinking about one's vocation, most people expect to get paid for their service. Dalton's only reward was another day of breathing and perhaps the knowledge that he had rid the world of one more source of evil. He thought of the old television recruitment commercials for the army, which proclaimed, "It's not just a job; it's an adventure." His life most certainly fit that description.

As if to accentuate that thought, the skull-shaped amulet hanging from his neck began to vibrate, but only slightly. Dalton looked around the busy diner, seeing that virtually every booth and table was occupied. He had never been attacked in broad daylight in all his years of hunting and slaying demons, let alone in a crowded restaurant, but something strange was about to happen, and he would be ready. However, Dalton had no way of preparing for what happened next.

Suddenly, everything in the room stopped moving, not just the people but everything. All sound ceased. There was no conversation, no rattling of utensils on plates, no distant classic rock coming from tinny ceiling speakers . . . nothing. Dalton discovered he could barely move, and attempting to do so took great energy. It was like one of those dreams where you try to run, but your feet feel weighted down by concrete.

He looked slowly around the room, which appeared to have been somehow stopped in time. He could scarcely believe his eyes. Agnes, the waitress who had just dropped his food, was frozen in the act of walking away. Her head was turned, looking back at Dalton with a seductive smile. Dalton looked down at her backside, caught mid-wiggle. It had been poetry in motion and now appearing as if in a photograph; it was Heavenly to behold.

But Agnes' picturesque posterior wasn't the strangest sight in the restaurant. A solitary fly hung in the air directly in front of Dalton as if caught in the same photographer's snapshot. Its wings were unmoving, yet it didn't fall to the ground.

"Quite an accomplishment, wouldn't you say?" A voice said from Dalton's right side.

In his peripheral vision, Dalton saw a form approaching.

"What's going on? What's . . . happening? Who . . . who are you?" Dalton asked as he slowly turned and saw the stranger standing beside him. He felt tense and wanted to be ready for battle, but that mysterious, unseen force hindered his movement.

The stranger was almost as tall as Dalton but not nearly as broad across the chest and shoulders. He appeared quite slim with none of Dalton's evident muscle tone. The man wore a white sports coat over a crisp white shirt and pants. On his head was an equally white top hat with a silver feather. His white hair stuck out from under the hat in places. The man's skin was pale and almost translucent, especially compared to his ruby-red lips. Dalton could tell the man's ghostly coloring was natural, not staged with lipstick and makeup.

"I suppose I should answer each of those questions, in turn, starting from the top. Don't you agree, Dalton?"

CHAPTER 12

"How . . . how do you know my name?"

"Well, now. I haven't even answered your previous three questions yet, and there you go, adding another one to the list. Oh well, let's take a stab at the first one, shall we? I believe that question was, 'What's going on?' Was it not?"

Dalton didn't respond; he just sat transfixed, unable to react. He was helpless. Dalton realized that if this creature was one of the higher-level demons Chang had warned him about, he was a dead man. This being could do whatever he wished to Dalton, and he was powerless to stop him.

"Well, now. What's going on is that I have momentarily stopped time for us to have a conversation. Actually, that's something of an oversimplification. You and I currently exist in a space parallel with what you think of as time. In other words, time is still marching on at a pace different from the current plane of existence. This action allows us to have a lengthy conversation here while scarcely a few seconds pass there. By the way, when things return to normal, your breakfast won't even have cooled, no matter how long this takes. Hopefully, that answers your initial question."

Dalton was dumbfounded, unsure if he understood what this stranger was saying. The man spoke impeccable English like an affluent person who had attended the finest schools and gotten a first-class Ivy League education. Dalton looked up and saw that the fly's wings seemed to have moved only slightly, but barely enough for him to have noticed. Dalton and this creature were operating at a different rate of time. He didn't know if this meant they were moving faster or slower than usual. Dalton decided it would be best not to overthink it but to go with the flow. Besides, he had no other choice.

The strange man continued, "Regarding your second question about what is happening, the answer is quite simple. You and I will have an essential and quite seriously enlightening conversation. Hopefully, you will be satisfied with the results when we finish."

"Well . . . that . . . was clear . . . as mud," Dalton tried to say sarcastically. He found he had to force out the words. It was as if the very act of speaking suddenly took more energy than he could muster.

"Perhaps so. Hopefully, things will come together and make more sense shortly. Now, onto the question of how I know your name."

"Wait a minute . . . you skipped . . . a question . . . who are you?"

The man chuckled, "Yes. I suppose I did and will continue to do so. That information is on a need-to-know basis, and you, my friend, do not need to know. However, rest assured that I am on the same side as you."

"So, you say . . . for all I know . . . you could be . . . a higher-level demon . . . one of those . . . Chang told me about."

"Yes, well, I can see why that might concern you. However, you can relax in that regard, Dalton. You see, if I were a demon, you would already be dead as you are essentially defenseless."

Dalton slowly shook his head in resignation as he tried fruitlessly to lift his arms. "I suppose you're right about that . . . ok . . . so what's . . . this discussion . . . we're supposed to have?"

Dalton managed to force it out. He found himself becoming angrier with this interloper by the second. Perhaps it was because of the man's superior and condescending attitude. Maybe it was because of Dalton's inability to defend himself.

The man—if he was a man—replied, "Well, Dalton. It's like this. We've been watching you and monitoring your progress over the past decade and have been pleased, if not amazed, by your accomplishments."

"We?" Dalton interrupted. "We as in . . .?"

"Those of us for whom such things matter."

"Vague as ever," Dalton said, feigning frustration. But he realized he was no longer concerned about this new companion wanting to harm him. Any creature capable of stopping time and rendering Dalton helpless had powers more extraordinary than he had seen so far from even the strongest demons.

CHAPTER 13

The strange being continued to smile at Dalton and said, "As I was saying, although we believe you've done an incredible job over the past decade ridding the world of demons, your powers are limited. You have the amulet, the Katana blades, your demon-free apartment, and all the glyphs and symbols necessary to protect you. However, as I demonstrated, they can do little to help against higher-level beings.

"Up to this point, we haven't found the need to intervene. However, after seeing the doppelganger demon Hell had decided to set upon you last evening, they're apparently stepping up their game."

Dalton asked, surprised to find the force slowing his speaking capability somewhat restored, "But why now? I mean . . . I've been doing this for more than ten years. Why didn't they do it sooner?"

The man seemed to contemplate his response, then said, "I suppose there are several possible reasons, none of which we may ever know. However, if I were to make an educated guess, one apparent reason is that time in the afterlife is irrelevant, unlike here on Earth. A decade here could be the blink of an eye in Hell, as could several millennia. Hell has many levels, all operating independently yet tied together. It's difficult to both comprehend and explain, especially to a mortal.

"Think of Hell like the structure of a major manufacturing corporation. If a worker on the manufacturing floor in Sandusky, Ohio, breaks a twenty-dollar tool, the corporate CEO in Dallas, Texas, will never hear about it. Nor might even the factory manager in the Ohio facility itself. However, the employee's immediate supervisor might learn of the incident and choose what action to take.

"Yet, although separate and independent, breaking that tool impacted the entire corporation in a small financial way. Of course, that twenty-dollar loss is unnoticeable in a multi-million-dollar corporate structure. Do you follow me so far?"

Dalton said, "Yes . . . I think I understand."

"So, we've determined that by breaking the inexpensive tool, the worker never found himself on the radar of the top corporate officials. His indiscretion likely didn't even make it to his boss's superior. But suppose he broke many, more expensive tools? Now, he would be getting noticed higher up the chain of command. What if he crashed a $500,000 machine, causing tens of thousands of dollars in damage and an equal amount of lost production revenue? His division would likely have to go to corporate headquarters for funds to repair or replace the machine. Do you see where I'm going with this, Dalton?"

"Yeah. I think so. I believe you're saying I'm like that worker. As long as I hunted and destroyed a few lesser demons, I went unnoticed, under the radar, as you said. These demons were from lower levels and were insignificant in the scheme of things. But each time I defeat a demon, Hell sends a stronger one, and I get noticed higher up the food chain." Dalton was surprised to learn his speaking ability had returned almost to normal. The creature must have done something to free it.

"Yes, Dalton. That's why you were forced to battle what was essentially a duplicate of yourself last night. Hell is patient. Hell is eternal. It watches and learns. Hell will keep sending stronger and stronger demons until they eventually destroy you."

"So why have they been screwing around with me for a decade? Why not just send a powerful demon right from the start and kill me?"

"Well, I suppose there's no kind way to say this. Did you ever see a cat torturing a cockroach? They like to pull off one leg at a time and make the creature suffer as long as possible. Hell is the cat, and you, my friend, are the cockroach."

"You're saying Hell has been playing with me up to this point. Now they're starting to get serious. Why me? Why not Master Chang? As far as I know, he never had to deal with a situation like this."

"That's correct, Dalton. Because as good as he might have been, Master Chang never posed the level of threat to the underworld that you do. You're special, Dalton. And, as I'm sure you learned last evening, Hell is watching you and learning how you think and act. They see you as a real threat, perhaps the only danger they've encountered in thousands of years by your time. That's why you're now on the radar of those higher up the ladder. It's also why I have been sent here."

Dalton thought for a moment, then said, "OK. I think I understand what you're saying. So, what do we do about it?"

CHAPTER 14

The man in white looked at Dalton for a few seconds, then spoke, "I'm somewhat embarrassed to say I haven't quite thought that through yet. You're a human, a mortal. You possess a great intellect, outstanding moral character, and incredible skills. However, the type of gifts I can bestow on you have never been given to a human before. These powers are not of your world."

Dalton said, "But I already possess this amulet, my Katana blades, and the magical etchings that protect me. So, you see, my power is already not only that of this Earth, and I think I might be ready to learn and use anything you offer me."

The strange man hesitated, then asked, "Did your Sensei tell you about the other amulet, which is the antithesis of the medallion you wear?"

"He told me a bit. He said it represents and supports evil and can take on different forms. Chang told me that in ancient Egypt, the amulet took the shape of a skull with ruby eyes mounted on top of a staff, wielded by an evil queen. He said it took various forms over the years, even recently appearing as a cell phone. If I recall correctly, he said it's a type of demonic tool. Its master can use it to open a direct portal to Hell. It opens a gateway by which demons and lower-level creatures can leave Hell and enter our world.

"The last Chang knew, The amulet was in the hands of a business executive known as R. John Showalter, or something like that, more than a decade ago. I asked Chang if the demons we battled might have come to Earth through a portal made by this evil amulet, and he said he didn't think so. He believed the demons that arise from the Earth to kill us are not being sent by anyone using the amulet. He felt lesser demons were sent to get us some other way."

"Well, Dalton. It appears your teacher was partially misinformed. It's not a surprise since all he knew was what he had figured out on his own over the years. He never advanced to a level requiring an appearance from myself or others like me. Over the millennia, the evil amulet has found itself in the hands of many different humans, either by design or accident. Whenever it does, the result is never good. As the adage says, 'Power corrupts. And absolute power corrupts absolutely.' That has been the case with the amulet. Eventually, every human who possessed the amulet and learned to use its power became corrupted until it became a catalyst for their destruction.

"The truth is, the power of the evil medallion is like that of an earthquake. When used to open a portal, it creates a series of aftershocks, mini quakes if you prefer. These can occur anywhere in the world at any time over any number of years. Remember I said there are no time constraints in Hell. A crack that opens to release a demon today may result from an act perpetrated by the amulet a thousand years ago. It was just waiting for the right opportunity."

"I'm confused. Why do the demons always show up where I am, and why do they always look for me and call me by name?"

"It, too, is a bit confusing to comprehend. These 'aftershocks' appear in the wake of a demon using the evil amulet. However, unlike actual aftershocks, they don't appear randomly. We'd have demons popping up and killing people everywhere if they did. These occurrences must have a purpose and a target. You were marked early on as a demon slayer. When that happened, you became a magnet for these incidents. In other words, these attacks could not take place without a purpose. Killing you is a purpose."

Dalton said, "So, if I had never helped Chang, was never marked, and he had died, then none of the demon attacks of the past decade would have occurred, right?"

"As far as you were concerned, they would not have happened. However, they most likely would have happened to some other person who was marked."

"So there ARE others out there doing what I do?" Dalton asked.

The man hesitated, then said, "I can neither confirm nor deny that statement."

"Can't or won't?"

"Both, Dalton. I can't, so I won't. You see, I don't have access to that information. I only learned about you and your demon-hunting skills recently. As I said, some things are on a need-to-know basis, and like you, if I don't need to know, I'm not informed. However, like you, I can logically deduce and assume there may be others even though I don't know definitively."

"Fine! Yet another non-answer. So, let's get to the part where you help me. That last demon they sent nearly did me in, and I'm not looking for a repeat performance."

"Very well. I think I know what I'll do. I noticed you are still wearing your wedding ring. How long has it been since your wife passed?"

"More than 12 years," Dalton explained.

"Yet you still wear your ring?"

"I haven't removed this ring since the day we were married, and I have no intention of doing so any time soon. It symbolizes my love for my wife, and her death has done nothing to change that. If anything, it has made that love stronger."

"Perfect. That was exactly what I was hoping to hear, Dalton. The power I will bestow upon you will reside within that wedding ring you wear and cherish so dearly. And it will only work for you."

"What sort of power will the ring possess? How will I use it?"

"It will have great power, power beyond imagining. Your mind and circumstances will determine what form that power takes and how it will be used."

CHAPTER 15

Dalton said, "Look. Don't think I don't appreciate all you're trying to do for me because I truly do. But I gotta say, you're starting to scare the crap out of me. I'm grateful for any additional help, but I don't want to be responsible for having too much power. As you said, I'm a human, a mortal. It's human nature to be flawed. I don't want to risk hurting innocents because I'm unsure how to control my newfound powers. I believe that falls under the category of letting a monkey drive your brand-new Mercedes."

"Not to worry, Dalton. It goes against your nature to harm innocents. You protect them with the same ferocity you use to fight evil. We believe you cannot be easily corrupted, if at all. As such, we feel confident you will never use this gift except in the war against the forces of Hell."

Dalton let out a sigh of resignation and said, "I appreciate your faith in me, and I promise I'll do all I can to use these gifts to fight the powers of evil."

"Then I suppose that's that," the strange man said.

Dalton uncertainly asked, "So when you do this power transmission thing, will there be thunder and lightning or maybe a Heavenly choir singing hallelujah or something like that?"

"Nah. I'm afraid that's way too Hollywood for a humble servant like myself."

"So when will I know you've done what you came to do?" Dalton asked.

The strange man smiled as he faded away, "It's already done."

CHAPTER 16

Suddenly, the silence was shattered by a cacophony of a million simultaneous sounds as time returned to normal. It was disconcerting, and Dalton jumped slightly at the shocking change.

"You ok, Doc, sweetie?" A voice called from nearby. It was Agnes, his waitress.

"Um, Yeah, Yeah, I'm just fine, Agnes. Thanks for asking. I was just deep in thought."

"Well, you best get to work on them eggs before they go cold on ya."

"Will do, Beautiful," Dalton said, giving her his patented wink."

Agnes returned his wink and wiggled along the counter, knowing Dalton's gaze was following her all the way.

Dalton thought, "I better be careful with my teasing that one, or my mouth might end up writing a check I have no intention of cashing."

He felt again for his wedding ring. Agnes was a sweet, attractive woman and only about six years his junior. She was also divorced multiple times and blatantly receptive to any advances he might decide to make. However, as far as Dalton was concerned, he had no interest in becoming physically or romantically involved with anyone at this or any future time in his life.

Besides his loyalty to Audrey, he could never risk the life of another because of his demon hunting. If he allowed himself to love again, Hell would find out, and that woman would become a target to be used against him. Dalton recalled how demons falsely claimed to have Audrey's soul many times and were torturing her, hoping Dalton would turn himself over to them. He could only imagine what they would do if he had a living person they could use against him. The possibilities were too numerous and too horrible to consider. He had to remain alone; he had no choice.

Dalton realized he was unconsciously touching his wedding ring. He noticed it felt slightly different in a way that was hard to explain. The ring still appeared to be a simple circular band of gold on the surface as it had always been. Yet somehow, it simultaneously felt like it was a living, pulsating entity. Whatever the strange man had done to the ring, he had definitely done something.

As he looked around the restaurant again, Dalton could not comprehend how all these people had been frozen in time, oblivious to his meeting with the white being, and now they were going about their business as if nothing had happened. Because as far as they were concerned, nothing did happen.

Dalton shook his head in amazement and proceeded to dig into his breakfast. His eggs were still hot, as the stranger said they would be. When he finished eating, Dalton left a twenty-dollar bill on the counter for a twelve-dollar breakfast as he always did, then headed toward the door.

Most regular patrons knew Dalton, if not personally, then by sight. They were used to his peculiar dress and paid little attention to him. None of them knew of his demon hunting and likely had no idea demons even existed. A couple of regulars gave him a casual nod in cordial recognition. A few strangers looked at him with sideways, distrustful glances as he passed them. Some involuntarily shuffled deeper into their booths, unconsciously inching away from the aisle.

Dalton ignored the strangers' stares, picked up his Katana blades, left the restaurant, and headed back to his apartment. He kept his head down on the way, paying little attention to anyone around him. As if he didn't have enough to think about, the white stranger had just given him more.

CHAPTER 17

The office of the president of Edmondson Systems in Yuengsville, Schuylkill County, Pennsylvania, sat empty. Its lavishly decorated interior boasted mahogany-paneled walls and highly polished Italian marble flooring covered by imported hand-woven rugs. A massive hand-made walnut desk was in the center of the room, designed and built by a team of craftsmen in Switzerland. Priceless works of art from many great masters adorned every wall.

During the previous five years, the company's aged owner and founder, T. Martin Edmondson, had miraculously transformed his already successful software company into a mega-conglomerate with offices and facilities worldwide employing thousands of workers. Observers had no idea how a man as old and apparently feeble as the reclusive Edmondson, who by rights should have been retired and in an old folk's home, had managed to pull off such an incredible accomplishment.

Despite the office's luxurious appearance, there was an underlying current of despair and emptiness accompanying the room. If one were to look closely at the carpet under the elegant desk, one would notice an unpleasant-looking dark stain. The rug was scheduled to be removed, as well as the leather desk chair, which bore a similar dark mark. These stains resulted from T. Martin Edmondson's self-inflicted knife wound.

The man had been found dead at his desk, and to call what he had done a knife wound was an understatement. The act had been much more brutal than one would have imagined. The old man had sawed and hacked away at his throat to the point that he had almost decapitated himself.

The company's future hung in limbo during the few days following Edmondson's demise. That was until it was discovered that just before Edmondson's death, he had merged his business with a company from the Midwest area of the country called Showalter Unlimited. This company was owned and operated by an equally reclusive billionaire known as R. John Showalter.

There was a dark secret surrounding Edmondson Systems. No one knew that the real T. Martin Edmondson had died six years earlier from a heart attack. During the first year following Edmondson's death, a demon known as Drabzat had been placed inside the old man's body until a suitable permanent replacement could be found. For the past five years, Edmondson's body had been inhabited by the essence of a man once known as Charles Wilson. It had been placed there by Showalter after he had used the evil skull amulet to sufficiently corrupt Charles Wilson's soul to make him Showalter's minion.

Charles Wilson had been a businessman working for Edmondson Systems, traveling on assignment in the Midwest. He had forgotten his cell phone the day he left and had to locate a temporary "burner phone." Unfortunately for Wilson, he found one in a strange eclectic store on the dark sidestreet. Unbeknownst to Wilson, Showalter had transformed the evil skull medallion into a bizarre-looking cell phone. It had skull-shaped keys with ruby eyes. Wilson soon accidentally discovered that the cell phone could be used to open portals to Hell from which demons could be called to do his bidding. As is always the case with uncontrollable power, Wilson soon became corrupted to the point where he would do anything to increase his strength and control, including murder.

Once Wilson had unwittingly accomplished everything Showalter wanted him to achieve, Wilson was sent into the bowels of Hell for what Showalter called appropriate orientation. Although only five minutes had passed on earth, thousands of years went by in Hell, during which time Wilson's soul was tortured and tormented in unimaginable ways. When Wilson was returned to this world, his soul was placed inside the dead body of T. Martin Edmondson, where it remained for the next five years. Wilson was forced to find ways to grow the business, which he had done remarkably well.

The problem was that Wilson found himself trapped inside the body of a walking-dead man. Although the body of Edmondson appeared relatively normal to outside onlookers, inside, Wilson had to live for five years with the stench of internal decay surrounding the decomposing creature he inhabited. Yet as repulsive as this was, for a time, Wilson knew it was better than the previous millennia he had spent in Hell being tortured. However, one day, when he could take it no longer, he snapped, and Wilson grabbed a knife and hacked at his throat in a feeble attempt to end his time of entrapment.

Although his near decapitation had succeeded in destroying the earthly body of T. Martin Edmondson, his soul was not freed. It went straight back to Hell, where it would begin suffering for eternity as Showalter had promised. Now was the time for the demon Showalter to return to earth and take his place as leader of his mega-corporation.

CHAPTER 18

Dalton walked slowly down the sidewalk. It wasn't very busy for eleven forty-five on a Sunday morning. Perhaps people were still at church, grocery shopping, or doing whatever normal folks did on such a day. As on mornings like this one, Dalton occasionally allowed himself to recall pleasant memories. He remembered sleeping in on a Sunday morning with his wife Audrey, then heading to their favorite local restaurant for a casual breakfast.

Such memories were bittersweet, as they brought him such joy on the one hand, while on the other, they filled him with gut-wrenching sorrow. Audrey had been much more than his wife; she was his everything. Now, all these years later, the pain in his empty heart was just as unbearable as it had been on the day she died.

"Remember all the good times we had on those Sunday mornings, Doc?" A soft, female voice called to him.

"What? Who was that?" Dalton called, placing his hand on the medallion around his neck. It wasn't vibrating, nor were its ruby eyes glowing. This sacred talisman didn't give a single warning of demonic danger. Yet, Dalton knew danger awaited him somewhere. He recognized the voice he had heard. It impossibly was Audrey's. Perhaps it was his imagination playing tricks on him or his need for a solid night's sleep. Dalton had learned over the years never to get comfortable with anything. In his life, even the most improbable could unexpectedly become a reality. He heard the voice again.

"Turn around, Doc, it's Audrey. Please, Honey, I don't have much time."

CHAPTER 19

In the corner of the empty office, something strange was occurring. The very fabric of reality began to shimmer and wave. A deep rumbling sound could be heard throughout the office while, in the middle of the air, a long slit began forming from a point about eight feet above the ground. The center of the slit started to spread open as a nauseating stench filled the room. From the bottom of the slit, dozens of steaming slime-covered tentacles flopped out side-by-side, creating a blanket of scorching writhing appendages, draping from the bottom of the portal to the floor of the office, forming a ramp of undulating flesh.

Then, two hands emerged from the center of the slit and began separating the opening, widening it to allow the exit of who or whatever was inside. The hands appeared to be normal human hands. As the slit widened, a man stepped from the opening and slowly walked down the carpet of slithering tentacles. The man was not affected by the searing heat generated by the appendages. He appeared to be a typical human male dressed in a dark business suit, blood-red tie, and dark slick-backed hair. The man was actually the demon, R. John Showalter.

"Oh Charles, oh Charles," Showalter said, looking around the empty room. "I had such hopes for you. You showed so much promise over the past five years. But I suppose all good things must come to an end." But of course, Charles Wilson couldn't hear Showalter's lamenting as he was too busy screaming in agony somewhere in the deepest chambers of Hell.

A few seconds later, the slit in the air opened again as a small hideous-looking demon slithered out, flopped to the floor then stood next to its master. The creature was about four feet tall, naked, and covered in slime. It had a pig-like snout, a mouth full of fangs, and two ram-like horns jutting back from its forehead. Its body was hairless save for a long mane extending from the top of its skull to the middle of its back.

"So Drabzat, here we are again. How long has it been?"

"Five Earth years, Master."

"It appears Charles Wilson has done all I ordered him to do. He has grown and merged the company with our parent corporation, Showalter Unlimited. I'm unsure why he chose to end his existence now when everything was going according to my plan."

"Stinky, smelly body," Drabzat replied.

"Seriously?" Showalter asked, "You honestly think that was why he chose to end it? Considering what he is going through now and will be for eternity, I think he would have been better off staying in the rotting corpse."

The hideous demon replied, "He probably couldn't take it any longer. Very stinky in there, Master. P-U!"

"Well, if you say so, Drabzat. After all, you would know that better than I do," Showalter said, then chuckled. "So, my loyal minion, it appears we need to get down to business and get this place back to running smoothly again."

Showalter grabbed onto the silver skull medallion with the ruby eyes dangling from the chain around his neck. He could feel it pulsing slowly and rhythmically. Its eyes were shining with a faint pink glow.

"We must get our house in order. I'll put a team of my earthly demons in charge and have this place running at full steam in no time. Then, once things here have been resolved, I plan to find the other amulet and destroy it, along with its troublesome master."

The short demon looked perplexed, "Other amulet, Master? I thought the one you commanded was unique."

"It is, Drabzat. But there exists another, similar but not exactly the same. In fact, it is the opposite of my incredible medallion in every way."

"Where do we find this amulet, Master?"

"I've learned it is owned by a self-proclaimed demon hunter who goes by the name Doc Dalton."

CHAPTER 20

Dalton spun around simultaneously, extracting both of his Katana blades. He had no idea why his pendant failed to warn him of the demonic threat, but there was no way he would tolerate some Hell-born scum distracting him with some false image of his beloved Audrey. They had attempted this ruse often in the past.

Dalton stopped in his tracks; his blades halted in the air just inches from the creature behind him. It wasn't a hideous slobbering beast, no monster, no demon. Although his mind could scarcely grasp what he saw, his beautiful Audrey stood before him. She looked even more radiant and lovely than she ever had in life. She was translucent, with flowing golden hair. She wore a long white gown that reached the sidewalk and seemed to billow in a breeze that Dalton could not feel.

"Audrey . . . baby . . . is that . . . really you?" Dalton asked, knowing it truly was her. He dropped his blades to the ground as his voice broke and tears streamed down his face. Dalton hadn't been in any way prepared for this. Was he really seeing what he thought he was seeing? What was she doing here? Why was this the first time she had appeared in so many years?

"It's me, darling," the image replied; her face was one of peaceful contentment. There was none of her mischievous earthly expression. She spoke in a soft, ethereal voice. It was then Dalton realized she was not speaking at all. The "voice" he heard was not coming through his ears but was manifesting inside his head. "My time here is short as it must be."

"Oh my God, Audrey, no, don't say that. It's been so long, Baby," Dalton cried.

"Not long . . . not on the other side."

Dalton recalled what the strange character had said earlier that morning in the diner. The man told Dalton that time on the other side was irrelevant. For all he knew, the past twelve years he spent suffering over the loss of his beloved Audrey might have been the equivalent of a few seconds for her.

"Audrey, Honey. Please, please take me with you. I'm ready to go. I want to be with you for eternity. I don't want to be here any longer. It's too much; it's too hard. I can't keep doing this. Please, baby."

Her peaceful expression never changed. The voice reverberating in Dalton's mind said, "I love you, Doc. And will forever, and you know that. But it's not your time. I'll wait for you. But you have things you must do, and you must live your life as it must be. I must go now, Darling."

The Audrey image started to fade, and as it did, Dalton heard her say, "Be careful, Doc, and watch out for the other amulet. It's coming for you soon."

"Nooooo!" Dalton cried as he fell to his knees, weeping. But Audrey was gone. A few people walked by, doing their best to cut a wide path around the large, sobbing man. It was not what they were accustomed to seeing in the morning on such a beautiful day. Dalton didn't care who saw him or what they thought. His heart ached so badly he could think of nothing else. Why couldn't she take him with her? Why must he continue living his miserable excuse for a life without his Audrey?

Then Dalton slowly began to rise to his feet. He tucked his Katana blades back into their sheaths and started walking. His head hung down in newfound sadness. Tears streamed down his face. He recalled the last thing Audrey had said to him. "Be careful, Doc, and watch out for the other amulet. It's coming for you soon."

The other amulet? Was that the same amulet Chang had mentioned to him? The same medallion about which the stranger in the diner was inquiring? Yes, it had to be—the evil twin of the amulet he now wore around his neck. But where was that silver skull pendant now? Still in the hands of an earth-bound demon named Showalter?

Surely, the amulet must have been passed on to someone else during the past decade. Then again, if time had no meaning on the other side, a decade meant nothing. Could the holder of the evil pendant travel back and forth between here and Hell? Could he appear at will in the past, the present, or the future?

It was mind-boggling for him even to try and consider these possibilities. Dalton was a simple man. He was ill-equipped for any such temporal considerations. All Dalton knew of space and time was what he had seen in sci-fi movies, which was very little. For the sake of his sanity, he decided that although the holder of the amulet might be able to move back and forth between Earth and Hell, perhaps the demon could not move into the past or future. This idea made sense to him. If the creature could go back in time, then he could have killed Dalton in the past before he ever became a demon hunter. It also made logical sense that if the demon couldn't go into the past, he wouldn't be able to go into the future.

But because time was irrelevant to such a demon, he could have crossed over into Hell more than a decade ago with the amulet; when he was ready, the monster could return to earth in the present time and use it against Dalton. He recalled how the man had said Hell was patient and time didn't matter to demons. He continued to try to reason out his situation. "That means that Audrey came to warn me that this devil, this Showalter, may have returned to earth, and if so, he is likely gunning for me."

CHAPTER 21

Drabzat was struck with a look of terror. "Did you say, Doc Dalton? You mean the same Doc Dalton who slew the invincible Fraggzzorr the Destroyer?"

"Yes, Drabzat. One and the same," R. John Showalter replied, "We almost took him out a few days ago with a special replicant demon we had created to destroy Dalton. This creature's skills were almost equal to his in every way."

"Almost?"

"Yes, my minion. Almost. Unfortunately, Dalton proved to be more clever than we had anticipated. Using some fighting techniques we had never seen him use previously, Dalton managed to destroy our demon," Showalter said with frustration. "We had been studying this Doc Dalton for a decade and thought we had incorporated all his skills into the doppelganger, but we were wrong."

Drabzat got a look of genuine fear on his hideous face, saying, "I have heard many tales about this Doc Dalton. He has become legendary among our people. It is said among my peers that Dalton cannot be killed. It is widely believed that his soul will never become ours."

Before the small demon realized it, an unseen force threw him against a far wall, and he felt dozens of his bones shatter into fragments. He collapsed to the floor in a broken heap of pain, his twisted limbs at unnatural angles.

Showalter roared, "Don't you ever say anything like that to me again, you miserable minion, or I swear by all that is unholy, I'll crush you from existence. Then I'll discard you like so much rubbish and find another slave to replace you before your soul makes it back to Hell."

"So . . . sorry . . . Master. I spoke out of turn. Please forgive me," the broken demon pleaded as he could feel his shattered bones beginning to heal. As agonizing as the process was, Drabzat knew this was a good sign. If his master allowed him to rebuild and had not yet sent him back to Hell for an eternity of torture, Showalter must mean to keep him, at least for now.

Showalter's anger began to fade, and he said in a calmer voice, "Very well then, Drabzat. I believe I will show you mercy this time, but only because I still have use for you. In fact, I have a new assignment for you."

"Anything, Master. Anything you command."

Showalter smiled his evil grin and said, "Well, Drabzat, my faithful servant. You will now have the opportunity to prove your love and loyalty to your master. You will destroy Doc Dalton and bring his amulet and soul to me."

CHAPTER 22

"But Master, how can I ever hope to defeat Doc Dalton when not only has he defeated the great Fraggzzorr, but also a special demon you created specifically to slaughter him?" The terrified demon asked as the last of his shattered bones knitted together.

Showalter smiled and said in a sly voice, "Surely, you don't give yourself enough credit, my humble slave. Are you not the right-hand servant to me, one of the most powerful demons Hell has ever produced?"

"Yes, Master. That is true."

"And are you not a shape-shifting wizard capable of assuming whatever form you choose?"

Drabzat said nothing as he was unsure what he should say. He may not have wanted to go against Dalton, but he had no desire to anger his master again and suffer those consequences.

Showalter continued, "Was it not you who took on the form of a lowly storekeeper to get the amulet in its cellphone incarnation into the hands of that mortal Charles Wilson."

"Um . . . yes, Master," Drabzat admitted reluctantly.

"And was it not you who transformed himself into that robber, lying in wait for Wilson outside the store? Using that assumed form, weren't you the one who first got Wilson to use the cellphone to inadvertently open a portal to Hell?"

"Yes, Master . . . That too was I."

"Of course, it was, my minion. Your powers of manipulation are legendary. That's why you hold such a high place as my servant. You have served me well in the past, and now you will have a chance at what will be your most incredible accomplishment. We have tried to defeat Doc Dalton with strength. We have tried duplicating his own skills, but nothing has worked. However, you can use your powers to fool Dalton long enough for him to leave his guard down. Then you will be able to destroy him."

Drabzat found himself loving his master's praises. Maybe Showalter was right. Perhaps he was not giving himself enough credit. He had accomplished many evil deeds for his master, things that not every demon could do. Maybe he was great enough to destroy this mere human, this Doc Dalton. The more he thought about it, the more he believed he had exactly what it took to get the job done.

Showalter, of course, knew the little demon had no chance whatsoever of defeating Dalton. He was to become nothing more than cannon fodder, a pawn in Showalter's game. However, although Dalton eventually would make minced meat out of Drabzat, the demon might survive long enough for Showalter to gather the information he needed.

The master had learned that the forces for good had intervened and had given Dalton some special powers. The burden fell upon Showalter to discover what those powers were and how dangerous they might be to Hell's plans. Showalter supposed he might have no choice but to battle Dalton himself at some time, but he hoped things would never come to that.

The only other way Showalter knew to learn the extent of Dalton's powers was to send a demon to battle him. He believed Drabzat had enough cunning and tricks to stay in the fight longer than most. If things went according to plan, Dalton would be forced to call on his newfound powers to defeat Drabzat, and Showalter would have the answers he needed.

Of course, Drabzat would be destroyed, and his soul would be cast into the great void, but sometimes sacrifices must be expected in war. Drabzat unknowingly would be the scapegoat necessarily made for Showalter's cause. The little demon was getting more excited by the second.

"I am ready, Master. When do you want me to slay this pretender, Doc Dalton?" Drabzat asked.

Showalter smiled his most devious grin and said, "Well, there's no time like the present."

CHAPTER 23

Dalton stood momentarily, staring at the empty spot where his beloved Audrey had appeared to him. She had been allowed to contact him, to warn him. Dalton wanted to see her again, and part of him hoped she might reappear if he stared and prayed hard enough. But he knew deep down inside that it would likely never happen again.

Whatever force allowed Audrey to appear would not do so any longer. Dalton's wife was dead, gone forever. Although he had accepted her death more than a decade earlier, he always felt she was nearby. It was an awareness that never left him until now. He suddenly felt more hollow, empty, and alone than ever.

After Audrey faded from sight on this street, Dalton sensed an absence in the very pit of his soul. It was like someone had reached into his chest and ripped out his heart. What remained was an emptiness a hundred times worse than what he had felt when she had died all those years ago.

Then Dalton realized he was wrong about his pain. Time had eroded his memories of that time and sanded down the jagged edges of his grief until today. Seeing Audrey again in all her beauty had been like a knife to rip open the wound of his grief anew. The effect caused his emotions to surface again and spill like blood from every fiber of his being.

Dalton knew Audrey didn't appear to cause him pain but to alert him of what would come. She came to warn him of the coming of the evil amulet. If there was one force in Hell Dalton had to be concerned about more than any other, it was that dreaded pendant. He supposed that was because Dalton knew so little about the thing. All he had managed to learn were various bits and pieces he had gathered throughout the years. But now, whoever currently possessed the pendant was apparently coming for him.

Dalton walked, still in a daze, trying to determine what steps he should take to prepare for the inevitable attack that surely was to come soon. As Dalton approached a side street, the amulet vibrated against his chest more violently than ever before. The tattoos bearing the various early-warning glyphs started tingling like dozens of insects crawling across his flesh. Dalton had never experienced any warnings to this degree of intensity before.

Then he heard a low humming sound, and Dalton realized his Katana blades were humming as if speaking to him in a song. But Dalton knew that tune very well. The blades and the other early warning systems told him trouble awaited him down that side street. It was unusual to find a demon attack late in the morning rather than in the dark of night.

Perhaps the monsters from Hell were getting bolder. Or, maybe they no longer needed to hide in the shadows of night. Possibly, they were ready to attack whenever or wherever they chose. Dalton didn't know why this was happening but was prepared for whatever awaited him. He turned and stood at the opening of the alley.

To his surprise, Dalton didn't see a giant crack in the earth spewing smoke and molten lava. Nor did he see the dozens of serpentine monsters crawling from a void. He saw no clone of himself waiting to duplicate his fighting skills. Also missing was any giant sword-wielding demon waiting to slice him to bits. Instead, all he found waiting was what appeared to be a feeble old man.

The old-timer wore a yellowed, stained athletic tee shirt, the kind young teenagers called "wife-beater" shirts, mottled with holes. The man was bald except for a thin white ring of disheveled hair, which formed a frizzled strip about the back of his head, connecting one of his oversized ears to the other. He appeared to be well into his seventies, if not his eighties, as his head was covered with age spots. Likewise, his skinny arms and hands were equally spotted and wrinkled.

The man's lips were thin and sunken inward, indicating that few, if any, teeth remained inside his shriveled mouth to help hold their recession at bay. His large eyes were sunken into his skeleton-like head, and dark semi-circular bags hung beneath them. The man's floppy ears dangled from his ancient skull, and Dalton suspected if he could see closer, he'd find tufts of coarse white hair sprouting from within them. The old man's nose was hooked and pointed downward, almost overhanging his upper lip. He sported a thick mustache and goatee that were uncombed and matted.

Dalton stood silently watching the old timer, certain there was more to the man than his first impression suggested; otherwise, his symbols would not have warned him. The man held something in his right hand, which he lifted and pointed forward so Dalton could see it better. It was some old and odd-looking cellphone.

Then again, odd-looking was something of an understatement. The phone was about two inches wide and four inches tall, blood red, with a row of gaudy sequins encircling the outside edge of the body. Dalton hadn't seen one of those dinosaurs for a few years before he started hunting demons.

The odd cellphone appeared to contain a simple viewing screen. Dalton saw the numeric buttons as large chrome keys shaped like skulls. The strange old man stood holding the phone and staring at him. Dalton suddenly recalled two things simultaneously. He remembered Chang telling him about the evil skull's last incarnation as a cell phone, just like this strange old man held. Then, he recalled his wife's warning that the evil medallion was coming for him.

Dalton prepared himself for whatever unexpected attack might be coming but decided to try to stall such an encounter until he knew more. He asked, "Who are you, old man, and what do you want of me?"

"Do you like my phone?" The man replied, wiggling the phone in front of himself in a playful, taunting motion while grinning an insane, almost toothless smile.

There was a madness in this old codger's eyes, the likes of which Dalton had never seen, even from that Baby Butcher Blake. Dalton said angrily, "Look, Pops. I ain't got time for these sorts of games. My time is valuable. Tell me what this is all about."

"It's about you, me, and this lovely cell phone," the old man replied, still grinning like a village idiot.

The silver skull amulet hanging against Dalton's chest vibrated even more, and his Katana blades hummed like never before. Dalton knew it was the strange cell phone causing the alert. He wondered if this old man might be the earthbound demon known as R. John Showalter, whom Dalton had been warned about.

Dalton asked, "Are you the demon known on Earth as Showalter?"

The old man just stood, smiling his ridiculous grin through his assortment of rotten and missing teeth, and said, "Me? Showalter? Don't be an idiot! No one ever warned me that the legendary Doc Dalton could be so stupid. What a pleasant surprise, however. No, Mr. Dalton. I am not Showalter. I am not fit to lick fungus from between the toes of such a great demon. I am the humble servant and slave to the incredible R. John Showalter. I am known as Drabzat. His greatness, Mr. Showalter, sent me in his place to kill you and take your soul."

"You? Kill me? You? Steal my soul? You are but a frail and obviously feeble old man. You are no match for me, Grandpa. Or should I say, Great-Grandpa?" Dalton chided.

The old man's grin grew wider, and his eyes bugged and glowed with insanity. If eyes were truly windows to the soul, then the look Dalton saw in this old man's eyes said his soul was a bottomless void. The old man said, "That's exactly what I hoped you would say."

Then, as the old man pressed a skull-shaped button on the cell phone, Dalton heard a cracking sound behind him. He turned and saw the air shimmer and then ripple like water on a pond's surface, changing before his eyes.

The old man began to change as well. He trembled from head to toe as his face reddened, and beads of sweat formed on his wrinkled brow. His eyes never left Dalton and seemed to bulge from their sockets as the man quaked violently. Dalton realized the old-timer calling himself Drabzat was no mere old man, no misguided human serving the powers of Hell, but a demon disguised as a human.

The creature was in the process of transforming into its true demonic form. Drabzat convulsed and twisted, stretching the muscles in his back and neck. He closed his bulging eyes tightly as he arched his head backward. Dalton saw two bumps appear on the front of the old man's forehead. They began to protrude and stretch the skin to the breaking point. The flesh ripped open, blood streaming down the man's face as a pair of horns emerged from the torn flesh. The horns grew rapidly longer, glistening with the old man's blood and then curling upward and back, resembling those of a ram.

The air around Dalton filled with a horrible stench, the likes of which he had never encountered: a combination of sulfur, human waste, dead animals, rotten meat, and God only knew what else. He glanced back at the rippling air current and could scarcely believe his eyes as a rip began to form in the very fabric of reality. The tear grew longer until it was almost eight feet long from top to bottom.

Dalton drew his Katana blades in preparation for battle. In front of him, the old man's mouth hung agape as his few remaining blackened teeth dribbled out, clattering onto the blacktop, bloody filaments dangling from their roots. Inside Drabzat's fowl cavern of a mouth, long, sharp fangs rose upward like stalagmites and downward like stalactites from the old man's puss-filled bleeding gums, replacing the missing teeth.

Behind Dalton, the crack forming in the air began to open at the center as long tendrils colored greenish-tan began to slither out of the ever-growing opening. Although the things were still several yards behind him, Dalton could already feel their heat. These snake-like creatures were larger and appeared even more savage than those he usually battled. He immediately understood that this portal to Hell could produce horrors worse than the typical openings he had seen so many times before.

Dalton looked back and saw the changing old man drooling maggots between his huge fangs. The worms slid down along a steady stream of bloody drool, congealing in his filthy beard. The man's hands had become much larger and grew huge razor-like talons. What had been an old man and was now a demon reached his arms high into the air. They were no longer aged and scrawny limbs but massive and undulating with rope-like muscles, drenched with glistening sweat. Dalton estimated the man had grown to more than twelve feet tall.

Dalton stood sideways between the demon Drabzat and the split in the atmosphere, trying to watch both simultaneously while preparing his attack strategy. Unfortunately, he had no way to plan how to defeat these dual attacks. He would fly by the seat of his pants in this battle. The crack had grown even wider in the middle, and more than a dozen now flailing tendrils were inching their way toward him.

Even with only the fleeting glances he could spare, Dalton saw these things appeared different than the snake-like creatures he typically battled, more than six inches in diameter, tapering down to two inches at their fronts and over ten feet long. Smoke arose wherever they contacted the asphalt as it bubbled and melted under their immeasurable heat.

Dalton stood with his feet planted firmly on the ground, one Katana blade pointing at the oncoming cluster of writhing tentacles to his right and the other aimed at the enormous demon to his left. Dalton still had no idea how he would battle both formidable foes simultaneously and thought he might be facing the end he had always feared for a moment.

CHAPTER 24

Dalton felt a vibration from the third finger on his left hand. It was his wedding ring. In the confusion of the attack, he had forgotten about the strange being who had supposedly given him some new power. However, Dalton had no idea what that power might be or how to use it.

He recalled what the man in white had told him, "It will have great power, power beyond imagining. Your mind and circumstances will determine what form that power takes and how it will be used."

That somewhat cryptic message provided him with no help whatsoever. Dalton still didn't understand what the man had meant but knew he needed something incredible to happen very soon, or he would never survive this attack. Then an idea came to him. Dalton envisioned an enormous blinding white light that would surround him like a second skin, a force-field of good against these forces of evil. He imagined an icy cold to counteract the demonic heat he was beginning to feel.

Dalton's wedding ring began to glow, and he felt an instant coolness coming from his ring finger. Then he saw an incredible white luminescence spread across his left hand, then up to his arm, until it rapidly surrounded his entire body. He looked at his arms still extended outward, swords at the ready, and saw them glowing with a white light brighter than he had ever seen. The light extended out from his hands, surrounding his Katana blades as well. Then, without warning, all the demons attacked as one.

The serpentine arms came at Dalton from the right faster than he would have believed possible. He barely had time to swing his sword when the things wrapped around his blade and right arm. Likewise, the monstrous demon Drabzat was on his side swinging what appeared to be an enormous spiked flaming war club. Drops of molten lava dripped from the swinging club, landing on the blacktop and turning it to burning tar.

The club missed hitting Dalton by a fraction of an inch, and he knew if he didn't find a way to control and magnify the power coming from his ring, he would die. Dalton thought again about the man who had bestowed the power on him and then about his Audrey. If he allowed these demons to beat him, his soul would be taken to Hell, never to be with his wife again.

The demon Drabzat pulled back the club, ready for another swing as the tendrils tightened their grip. Several of the things had wrapped themselves around his neck, squeezing and cutting off his oxygen supply. Dalton knew if it weren't for the power he had gotten so far from the ring, the serpentine vines would have burned right through his flesh and severed his head. As things were, Dalton could feel himself getting hotter by the second and could scarcely catch a breath. One of the tendrils appeared in front of Dalton's face, and he could see a rudimentary mouth at its end filled with thousands of needle-like teeth.

As Drabzat began to take his next swing, Dalton understood he would not have been given any power that would allow him to be beaten so easily. He mustered all his inner strength and focused on the coldest cold he could imagine. His right sword glowed even brighter than before, as did his entire body. Dalton slowly swung his sword with great effort, and the blade cut through the tendrils holding him.

He felt his wedding band vibrate, and a giant beam of light shot out of his fingertips and hit the oncoming club mid-way to striking. The club stopped in its path. Drabzat pulled back his hands in pain and stared helplessly as he dropped the now-frozen weapon. It fell to the ground and shattered into an incalculable number of fragments as if dipped in liquid nitrogen.

Dalton was as much in shock as the demon was. Drabzat stood in stunned silence, staring at his now frozen hands. But that wasn't the end of the monster's troubles. The luminescent cold was rapidly spreading up his wrists to his massive forearms. Dalton looked back at the serpentine creatures and saw them retreating into the portal, leaving their frozen, severed remnants behind. The pieces lying on the ground collapsed into mounds of crystallized ice dust.

The demon screamed in agony as the ice spread throughout his body until the glowing cold reached his head, and all sound ceased. Dalton swung his Katana blades, striking the frozen monster, and the demon crumbled into the same icy dust as the tendrils had. Dalton saw the strange cell phone the demon had used to open the gateway lying on the ground. He lifted his swords, determined to bring them down on the thing and destroy it.

However, that was not to be. As Dalton watched in amazement, the cell phone reverted to its original form. A shining silver skull medallion, the exact size and shape of his talisman, floated in the air a few feet before him. Although it was an almost perfect doppelganger of his medallion, this evil pendant was smooth without a mark, etching, or glyph.

The skull hovered for a few seconds before it flew backward into a small slit that seemed to appear in the air out of nowhere. When Dalton looked at the serpent portal, he was astonished to find it gone. He looked back at the smaller portal into which the evil amulet vanished and saw it, too, had closed and disappeared. In his mind, Dalton heard a soft, educated-sounding voice.

"Nice work, Mr. Doc Dalton. Very impressive. Drabzat was a worthy foe, yet you bested him. That was certainly an interesting new weapon you've added to your arsenal. I'll be sure to remember that. Maybe next time, I'll challenge you myself. Perhaps not. I suppose time will tell."

Then, the strange voice was gone. Dalton thought, "The demon, the one they call Showalter. It must have been him."

Dalton looked at the shattered remnants of demonic flesh that littered the area. As he watched, He saw the particles turn to dust and blow away in a sudden wind. Nothing remained of the battle that had ensued except for Dalton's uneasy feeling that he hadn't seen the last of that evil skull amulet. He also suspected that someday he would have to encounter Showalter face-to-face.

CHAPTER 25

The remainder of Dalton's walk home to his apartment went without incident, for which he was grateful. After the trials of the previous thirty-six hours or so, uneventful was precisely what he needed. He had a lot to ponder, and the only place Dalton could hope to accomplish this was within the safe confines of his apartment.

Dalton sat in his recliner and allowed his mind to drift back to his first battle two nights earlier with the demon, Fraggzzorr the Destroyer, the former murdering pervert Edmund Carlton Blake, also known as Baby Butcher Blake. Usually, there was little or no conversation when Dalton was fighting these Hell-spawned creatures. There was never usually time for banter or clever retorts; all the energy went into the battle. However, this demon chose to goad Dalton to push him emotionally as if testing his ability to focus.

The more he thought about it, the more Dalton realized why Hell had sent the vile creature Fraggzzorr. It wasn't just to destroy Dalton. Hell likely knew Dalton could beat the demon. The attack was to watch Dalton and study his reactions to stimuli, not just fighting but verbal assaults. Perhaps Hell was monitoring the conflict to learn which of Dalton's emotional buttons to push. Fraggzzorr served that purpose nicely.

Then Dalton understood that the latest Demon he fought, the one known as Drabzat, was sent for a similar purpose. The creature challenged Dalton's skills and allowed Hell to have a front-row seat at a demonstration of his newfound abilities. He wondered what that would mean for him in the future. Would Hell devise a way to defend against his freezing light? Then he questioned if that power might be the only power the ring produced, or were there more?

The man in white had said that when the need arose, the ring would do whatever Dalton needed. He said, "It will have great power, power beyond imagining. Your mind and circumstances will determine what form that power takes and how it will be used." That was what had happened during the battle. Dalton needed to cool the blazing Hellfire, and his ring had handled that problem nicely.

Although that was all well and good, Dalton knew he would feel much better if he had a more thorough understanding of all his newfound powers. Although he believed the man had spoken the truth, Dalton couldn't afford to take a risk like that. He had to know and would need to test his new abilities.

Unfortunately, the only way to do that was in battle. Those battles would come; eventually, they always did. But for now, after the several hectic days he had experienced, a nap was definitely in order. Dalton looked at his wall clock and saw it was three o'clock in the afternoon. He closed his eyes, and before he even realized it, he was fast asleep.

CHAPTER 26

Dalton opened his eyes, looked again at the clock on the wall, and saw it was seven o'clock.

"Wow! I can't believe I slept for four hours. I never nap that long," Dalton said to himself. Then he noticed bright rays of sunlight between the closed, room-darkening shades. "Woah. Wait a minute. It's not seven at night; it's seven in the morning! Holy crap, sixteen hours! I know I've never slept that long before."

That was when Dalton realized just how exhausted he must have been. He wondered if his age was catching up with him. He had never been so tired before. Then, he questioned whether using his new power had caused him to be so weary. Could this new power put a previously unknown drain on his energy? This would be another thing he would have to watch out for. However, for the moment, the rumbling in his stomach was telling him it was time for breakfast.

"The body needs what the body needs," Dalton said to the empty bedroom. "And right now, this body needs some serious nutrition, as in a seriously large breakfast."

After completing his morning ritual, Dalton returned to the same diner where he had breakfast the previous day. Then again, that was where he had breakfast almost every day. It just felt a bit weird as Dalton walked into the diner. This was apparently because he had slept so long; it seemed he had just left the restaurant. As he took his place at the counter, Dalton wondered if the strange man in the white suit would make another appearance, but thankfully, he did not.

"Morning, tall, dark, and a wee bit scary," the curvaceous waitress, Agnes, said as she placed a glass of water before Dalton. "You're looking one heck of a lot better today than you did yesterday, Sweetie. I'm glad to see you got yourself some beauty sleep. Not to suggest that you needed beauty sleep. Uh uh, not one bit at all."

Dalton smiled, "I see what you're doing there, Agnes. You're trying to butter me up to get a big tip." No sooner had the words left his lips than Dalton realized he had just handed the waitress an opening to take his words, twist them into something sexual, and send them right back at him, which she did almost immediately.

Agnes winked and smiled seductively, then said, "Honey, if I butter you up, it'll be like buttering a cinnamon bun; believe me, I won't settle just for a big tip. I'll want the whole thing!"

Dalton felt the blood rush to his face as he blushed with embarrassment. He should have known better than to play these games with Agnes. She had been around the block more times than most and could get down and dirty with the best of them. Dalton recalled how a busboy at the restaurant had once told him, "Look, Doc. You might be one big tough guy, but you ain't no match for Agnes. You best be careful around that one. If she gets her hands on you, she'll swallow you up and spit you out bald."

Dalton had no idea what that expression meant, but he didn't like how it sounded and had no desire to find out. Agnes was nobody's fool. She knew what she wanted and wasn't shy about going after it. It appeared Doc Dalton might have been at the top of her want list. Dalton found it strange how he had no trouble battling every form of demon Hell could throw at him with not an ounce of fear. But sometimes, Agnes scared the living crap out of him.

He took a gulp of his water to buy himself some time, let out a deep sigh, and then said, "Ok, Agnes, I surrender; you win. Now, how about you get me my regular breakfast."

"No problem, Doc, Honey Pie. One big, strong, hungry man breakfast coming right up."

Doc said nothing more, just nodded his head as she walked away. He recalled the previous morning and how everything had frozen in time when the strange character came to tell Dalton about his new power. It gave Dalton a peculiar feeling looking around at people going about their normal, everyday lives, oblivious of the war between good and evil going on around them every day, a war Dalton had to fight on their behalf, as much for them as for his own survival.

Sometimes, that train of thought angered Dalton. It was because he risked his life and his immortal soul every week fighting the demons of Hell. But these people, these so-called normal people, were clueless. Dalton also knew that many people he fought to protect thought him strange and perhaps odd because of how he dressed. However, this was Dalton's life. He was a demon hunter, whether he liked it or not.

A few minutes later, Agnes returned with his food and set everything before him, interrupting his thoughts. She said, "Well, Doc Honey, I can see you're deep in thought. Solving all the world's problems, are you?"

"Yeah . . . something like that."

"Well, Sugar. That's what we pay them ridiculous politicians to do. You gotta take care of yourself, and the rest of the world be damned."

Dalton thought about her last statement and had to suppress a chuckle. If she only knew how he was the only thing standing between humanity and soul-sucking damnation.

"You best be eating them eggs before they get cold."

"Right you are, Agnes," Dalton said, happy to get Agnes deflected from her endless barrage of sexual innuendos.

Then she looked at him again with that come-on-over-here-and-get-yours look and said, "And you know, Doc. When you're ready for dessert, I've got something really sweet in store for you. All you have to do is ask."

Dalton stammered clumsily and said, "Um . . . ah . . . thanks, Agnes. I'll keep that in mind."

"You be sure to do that, Sweet Cheeks," Agnes said as she wiggled along the serving counter.

Dalton thought to himself, "Oh, Dalton, my boy. You'd better watch yourself. That woman is a wild one."

CHAPTER 27

As Dalton finished his tea, he had a weird sensation, Like he was being watched. He wasn't receiving warning signals from his amulet, so he knew no supernatural danger was nearby. Yet that strange feeling wouldn't go away. As usual, his Katana blades were in the closet at the front of the diner, but he had several smaller knives easily accessible inside his coat. Dalton hoped he wouldn't have to use them in the busy restaurant, but if he did, he would be ready.

Since there were no stools at the counter to his left, Dalton looked to his right and saw a slightly built, bespeckled man sitting on a stool one away from his, darting his eyes first toward Dalton, then away from him with what looked like a combination of, fear, awe, admiration, and possibly hope. The guy seemed harmless at first glance, but as Dalton understood, one could never be too careful.

Dalton didn't say a word. Instead, he scrutinized the man from head to toe with his peripheral vision while never taking his eyes off the man's hands. Dalton had learned to trust his gut when it came to first impressions. The stranger looked like an accountant, stopping for a quick breakfast before heading to work. The would-be accountant wore black dress pants, shiny black wing tips, and a short-sleeve white open-collar dress shirt.

If Dalton were to rethink his assessment, he'd change his initial impression and tag this character as more of a Jehovah's Witness than an accountant. Whatever his profession, this guy seemed to be no threat to Dalton or just about anyone else on the planet.

The man locked eyes with Dalton and then stared back, mouth agape, for a few seconds. Then, very quickly, the man's eyes seemed to snap to alertness. The small man slid to the stool next to Dalton before Dalton realized the man had done so. He stuck out his hand, apparently hoping for Dalton to shake it. Dalton glared at the man with his patented icy sub-zero stare.

In a timid voice, befitting his appearance, the man managed to squeak out, "You're Mr. Dalton . . . Doc Dalton, are you not?"

The man had pulled back his previously offered hand as if he were afraid the giant, wild-looking Dalton might tear off his arm and beat him to death with the bloody end of it. If he truly knew Dalton, he would know that scenario was not as far-fetched as one might initially believe.

Dalton took another few seconds to burn holes in the man with his antisocial glare, then said, "Who wants to know?"

The little man looked perplexed. His eyes blinked behind his coke bottle glasses, then said, "Well, I suppose . . . I do. Isn't that obvious?"

Dalton wasn't sure if this guy was serious or not. Under normal circumstances, a little guy like that asking such a conde-scending question of someone Dalton's size was akin to thumb-ing your nose at an enraged grizzly bear. Neither of those actions was destined to end well. But something about this man told Dalton to listen to what he had to say.

The man stuck out his hand in greeting a second time, then said, "I'm Wilbur, Wilbur Fernwood. I'm happy to make your acquaintance, Mr. Dalton."

Dalton stared at the man's outstretched hand but didn't take it. Once more, the man pulled back his hand uncomfortably. Dalton looked coldly at Fernwood but said nothing.

Fernwood was now breaking out in a sweat as he tried to come up with the right words. In hushed tones, the man said, "Um . . . I . . . ah . . . I've been told, Mr. Dalton, that you are . . . well . . . a demon hunter."

This took Dalton aback for a moment. He knew people found his dress and persona somewhat unconventional, but he didn't think anyone knew of his demon-hunting activities. He had taken great pains to ensure his secrecy. Probably 99 percent of the population weren't even aware that demons existed, let alone that people like him hunted and destroyed them.

Dalton finally spoke, "Sorry man, you got bad info. I ain't what you think I am. Wherever you're getting your info, it's wrong."

"I got the information from my daughter," the man said, appearing to fight back the tears. "Her name is Elsa. She's only fourteen."

"I don't know, no Elsa, and I surely don't hang with 14-year-old girls. That would make me a different sort of person entirely, which, by the way, I'm not either."

The man hesitated, looked around the diner, then whispered, "You don't understand, Mr. Dalton. I really need your help. I'm desperate." He pulled out a wallet thick with one hundred dollar bills and said, "Look, I can pay you whatever you want. I have lots of money, but it means nothing if Elsa is . . . well, how she is."

Dalton was starting to get curious. Not that he wanted the man's money. He had plenty of money of his own. However, the fact that this guy was willing to give up a wallet full of hundreds told Dalton the man was obviously very serious and desperate. He asked, "You said you need my help, and your daughter, Elsa, is sick. How sick is she? I mean, despite my nickname, I'm no doctor. What's wrong with her?"

Fernwood looked around, hesitated, then said, "If I were talking to anyone else, I would be careful about what I said out of fear of sounding like a raving lunatic. But if you are what I believe you are, you'll understand. Somehow, some sort of demon has taken possession of my baby girl. It controls her body, using her to communicate with us like its puppet. The last thing the demon asked for was you, and it called you by name."

"Look pal, even if you think I'm some superhero demon hunter, I don't know Jack squat about demonic possessions, exorcism, or anything like that. I think you need to speak with a priest or somebody. I'm not the one you want, especially if your little girl's life depends on it."

The man pleaded with tears rolling down his cheeks, "Please, Mr. Dalton. This demon said unless I come and get you, he would make my little girl kill herself. Then he said he would move on to another child, then another, until you eventually would have no choice but to come."

Dalton looked around the diner. He didn't want this joker attracting unwanted attention. Dalton loved this place, especially for breakfast, but if people started making a fuss about him and his causing a disturbance, he wouldn't be welcome here for long. Dalton grabbed the man by the arm and, after leaving a twenty-dollar bill on the counter, picked up his Katana blades from the front closet and led the weeping man out of the diner as incon-spicuously as possible.

Once they were outside and around the corner out of sight, Dalton grabbed the small man by the front of his shirt, got within an inch of his face, and said through gritted teeth, "Look, you little weirdo freak, I have no idea who you are or who you think I am, but nobody gets away with harassing me at my favorite breakfast place, *capisce?*"

The man looked terrified and said, "Oh . . . oh yes . . . I'm . . . I'm so sorry, Mr. Dalton. I only came because I was ordered to tell you about my daughter's horrible situation. Please, please, I'm begging you, sir. Will you at least come to see my little girl? If you don't, he'll kill her. What's worse is I think her immortal soul will be lost in Hell for eternity."

Dalton hesitated for a moment. Something felt definitely hinky about this, but none of his warning signals were alarming. His amulet wasn't vibrating, nor were his Katana blades. That meant this Fernwood guy was a human and not a demon. But Dalton had never encountered any situation like this before.

He asked, "Ok, Wilbur, run this by me again only slowly. I want to hear it again before I make up my mind."

Fernwood took a deep breath and said, "A few days ago, my daughter, Elsa, started acting strange. She was argumentative about everything and just seemed angry all the time. I blamed it on teenage girl hormones. You know how young girls can be."

Dalton had no idea how young girls acted, as he had no offspring. But to keep the man talking, Dalton said, "Um . . . yes, yes . . . I know what you mean."

The man said, "Well, after a day or so, it was clear that Elsa was no longer in control of herself. That was when the demon spoke to me for the first time."

"Ok, so tell me what this demon said," Dalton prompted.

"The demon said his name was Zartrog, and he was sent to occupy my daughter to kill a demon hunter. I was already having a hard time wrapping my head around the idea of a demon speaking to me through my daughter, let alone believing there were demon hunters out there. This morning, he told me your name is Doc Dalton. He told me where to find you and said if I came back without you, he would force my Elsa to slice herself to pieces."

Then the man broke down, weeping uncontrollably. Dalton stood and looked at him, unsure what to do about this situation. He said, "Put your wallet away. I don't want your damn money. I'll make a deal with you. I'll examine your daughter and determine if your words are true."

"I swear, Mr. Dalton, I'm not lying to you."

"Relax, Wilbur. I believe you're telling me the truth, at least as you see things, but that doesn't mean what you see is true. It would be best if I make that determination myself."

Wilbur said, "Fine. That's all I asked. I was told to bring you to this demon, and if I did, he said he would let Elsa go. "

Dalton said, "I need you to understand a few things before we move forward. If this demon is real, there's no guarantee he will let your daughter go, regardless of what he told you. He is a demon, a minion of the great deceiver himself. Lies are as natural to demons as breathing is to you and me."

"Ok, Mr. Dalton. I understand."

"And there's one other thing," Dalton said.

"What's that?"

"If you've lied to me or your situation is anything other than what you profess, you'll have to deal with me personally. Trust me, Wilbur, you don't want to be on my bad side; it's extremely unhealthy for you. Do I make myself clear?"

The man looked like he was on the verge of passing out but managed to hold himself together and say, "Yes . . . yes, I understand."

CHAPTER 28

"Oh, Drabzat, poor Drabzat," R. John Showalter said to the empty room as he paced back and forth in his executive office at the former site of Edmonton Systems, now known as the East Coast Headquarters for Showalter International. He was a demon with many problems on his overflowing plate and often spoke aloud like this to help sort through important issues.

As he walked around the office, Showalter held the sacred skull amulet in his right hand. It had returned to him through a portal shortly after Drabzat had been destroyed. Now, he held it tightly in his hands, feeling the comfort its presence brought him. Showalter had been the pendant's master for several hundred Earth years, but the amulet had many masters before him, as it had been around for thousands of centuries in one form or another.

Showalter said, "Drabzat, my poor vanquished minion, you may have perished in your attempt to kill Doc Dalton, but your sacrifice was not in vain. Thanks to you, I could witness the special new power given to Doc Dalton. More importantly, I discovered the location of the source of that special power. It was quite a clever trick, hiding it within Dalton's wedding ring. The man never takes the wretched thing off for any reason.

"I must admit, that icy blast was quite effective. It may have originated in that ring, but Dalton used his mind to make it real. I found it very clever how he turned poor old Drabzat into a frozen popsicle. I must learn more about what that new power can and can't do. The white beings have taken a big chance by putting such incredible power into the hands of a mere mortal. I have often seen how humans fail miserably once given god-like powers. Then again, humans can't help but fail, being the flawed creatures they are. If that weren't true, I suppose I might find myself out of the soul-stealing business."

Showalter laughed aloud, his chuckles echoing off the walls of the empty office. "So now it appears I have much work ahead of me. My first order of business will be to find myself another minion. Drabzat may have been subpar in many ways, but he could be quite clever when he put his mind to it. His shoes will be difficult to fill.

"In the meantime, it will be interesting to see how the latest challenger, demon Zartrog, does against Dalton. If I must say so, this latest approach was quite clever in its originality. I honestly don't know why I didn't think of it sooner. I mean, what all-American demon-hunting superhero can pass up the chance to save a poor, defenseless teenage girl? Even though he knows nothing about dealing with demonic possession, it appears that Dalton is willing to take the bait. Unfortunately for him, I know something he doesn't know, and that bit of information will be his downfall."

CHAPTER 29

Dalton walked with Wilbur Fernwood for seven blocks to the man's brownstone. The home was in a formerly bad section of the city that had undergone something of a rebirth over the past decade. Most of the rundown, abandoned row homes had been sold for pennies on the dollar to investors willing to take a risk and pump money into gentrifying the several-block area. It had apparently been a success, judging by the immaculate condition of the refurbished homes.

"So, Wilbur. What exactly do you do for a living anyway? This neighborhood is a lot more upscale than I had expected," Dalton asked.

"Me? Oh, I'm just a boring old accountant for a company downtown."

"Ding ding!" Dalton thought, "My first guess was correct! Give that demon hunter a Cupie Doll."

Wilbur said, "I took a chance about nine years ago and bought one of these brownstones. It was a real dump when I bought it. But because I was able to snag it for a song, I could afford to spend some money to refurbish it. My wife and I originally planned on flipping the place and making a killing, but we fell in love with the area and decided to stay. Our initial investment has quadrupled in value, not that I would ever consider selling. Especially not since . . ."

Dalton saw the sadness in Wilbur's face and asked, "Not since what, Wilbur?"

The man's reply was delivered with a quivering voice, "Not since my wife, Jenna, passed away last year. It was devastating for my daughter and me; to be honest, we finally began getting our lives back on track when this demonic creature showed up. Jenna and I had fixed up the house together over many years, and it has too many fond memories for me to consider leaving. That's another reason I need to rid my Elsa of this demon. If anything happened to her, on the heels of losing Jenna, I think I would die. I know I would want to. Mr. Dalton, we need this demon gone so we can go back to trying to rebuild our shattered lives."

Dalton understood all too well what Wilbur was saying, having been through his own loss. He said, "I understand where you're coming from, Wilbur, more than I care to explain. Let's go inside and see what I can do for you."

The two walked up the stone steps to the gorgeous glass and hardwood front door. Wilbur turned the front door knob, opening the door for Dalton, who then led the way. The two men stopped at the base of a long flight of polished oak stairs leading to the second floor. The front door suddenly slammed shut behind them, and Wilbur jumped with fright. Dalton heard the lock engage. Wilbur stood right behind him, wide-eyed with terror.

"What the Hell was that?" Wilbur asked.

Dalton lifted his head as if sensing something in the air. The skull medallion vibrated rapidly against his chest as its ruby eyes glowed brighter than ever. The etchings on his Katana blades pulsed red. Dalton said, "It looks like we're about to find out, Wilbur."

A demonic, multi-octave voice, sounding like a dozen insane people shouting simultaneously, traveled downward from above. "So I see you did as I commanded, Wilbur Fernwood. You brought my quarry to me. That is you, Doc Dalton, legendary demon hunter, is it not? Of course, it is. I can smell your stinking soul; it is marked for death by Hell itself. Well, today is your most unlucky day because death is the only thing you will be enjoying today, and I will be bringing it to you. Why don't you come up here and see what I have waiting for you, Dalton? It will be something you've never seen before. Come up and face me, mortal coward; I'm waiting."

Dalton looked at Wilbur and asked, "Is that the voice that commanded you to come for me?"

"Yea . . . yes . . . it is. But now, it no longer sounds anything like my baby girl, Elsa. But as you'll soon see, the demon Zartrog controls her now."

Dalton cautiously began climbing the stairs, one at a time. As he did, the temperature seemed to be getting cooler with each upward step. Wilbur walked behind him, carefully staying a safe distance back. He was not ashamed to admit he was no hero. When Dalton reached the upstairs hallway, the temperature around him suddenly dropped at least thirty degrees. He saw his breath form steam with each exhalation, and icy air entered him with every inhalation.

"Perhaps you should wait here," Dalton told Wilbur.

"Believe me, going in that room is the last thing I want to do, but I have no choice. My baby girl is in there."

"Very well, but be sure to stay behind me."

"I most certainly will. Believe me, that won't be a problem," Wilbur replied.

With Wilbur behind him, Dalton walked down the hall toward the room at the end. As he approached the open door at the end of the hall, Dalton looked from side to side, noticing frost, then ice forming on the expensive wallpaper and carpeting. This really was something he had never witnessed before, and he was unsure what to expect. His previous demonic encounters always involved fire, molten asphalt, and flaming demons. This was going to be a whole new ballgame. Never before had he felt such utter and debilitating cold.

Dalton walked into the bedroom and head-on into a horror beyond any conjured in his most terrifying nightmares.

CHAPTER 30

Dalton didn't know what he had expected to see, perhaps a young girl resembling Linda Blair in a scene from The Exorcist. However, on the bed, he saw no young girl with a 360-degree rotating head or pea-soup-colored projectile vomiting. To his surprise, there was no sign of a young girl anywhere.

A monster occupied the bed, a beast hideous beyond imagination. The large mattress was covered with a gelatinous creature appearing to be made up of dozens, if not hundreds, of long, slime-covered tentacle-like appendages. The bed and the demon in it were the only things in the room not covered in thick layers of glistening ice. The area of the ceiling above the bed had long, dripping icicle stalactites, which had been formed by the heat rising from the monster on the bed.

Dalton thought, "So this demon is a fire demon like all the others, after all." But then he realized that wasn't exactly true. Although this beast radiated heat, Dalton had never encountered any demons that could survive in such frigid conditions. Whenever he met one in the winter months, the creatures would come with more heat and flames than was typical to clear a way for them through snow and ice.

Then Dalton recalled how he had created such frigid conditions only a few hours earlier with his new special power and had used it to destroy the demon Drabzat. Perhaps that was why this current situation existed. It was apparent that the forces of Hell were still studying him and learning. Using a monster unaffected by the cold made it useless for Dalton to try that same trick again.

Dalton had also never seen any demon that looked as hideous as this monster. The creature's continuous writhing, pulsating, and almost liquid undulating flesh made it impossible to determine its exact appearance. As best as Dalton could tell, the thing was a mound of constantly moving slime-covered fleshy tentacles sprouting out from a round, dome-like outcropping near the center of the bed. The thing had dozens of eyes that seemed to float haphazardly in the gelatinous dome, which Dalton thought of as its head.

Then Dalton realized the significance of the one thing he had failed to notice missing from this twisted tableaux: the young girl, Elsa. Had this vile demon taken over the poor girl's body so completely that she no longer existed? Then he suddenly understood, a second too late, why there was no longer a helpless girl present. It was because there never had been any girl. This was all a lie, a trap.

Dalton felt an incredible shock impact him from behind, and the pain was so great it made him think his head would explode. All of his muscles began to twitch and spasm. As he collapsed to the floor convulsing, he heard that same multi-octave demonic voice shouting, "That's enough, Fernwood, my minion, you brought him to me and disabled him. I don't want you to kill him. That pleasure must be all mine."

"Yes, Master Zartrog. I will do as you command," Wilbur replied, his head appropriately bowed in supplication. He dropped the taser gun to the floor, and Dalton slowly and painfully began to feel as if he could breathe again. Although his thoughts were still scrambled, his brain started comprehending what had happened.

Wilbur Fernwood didn't have a daughter, and this probably wasn't even his home. If that was his actual name, Wilbur was a human servant for this demon called Zartrog. Because Fernwood was mortal, his medallion hadn't alerted Dalton. But this Wilbur character was evil. He might be human, but he was still evil. Why hadn't his amulet sensed the man's evil? Chang had warned him about such minions, but this was the first time Dalton had encountered one. And judging by how badly things were going so far, it might be the last time he would ever be battling anyone.

CHAPTER 31

Suddenly, Dalton was lifted into the air by an unseen force and slammed back against one of the ice-covered walls. He hung suspended several feet off the ground with his arms and legs splayed, forming an "X." The cold rapidly found its way through his layers of clothing to his back, and Dalton could feel his core body temperature drop rapidly toward the danger zone.

"You thought yourself rather clever using your newfound powers to destroy my friend Drabzat with cold, didn't you, Dalton? Such a horrible and frigid end for such a noble demon. However, as you can see, the cold does not affect me. You will also discover it's not so pleasant to be on the receiving end of an icy death. And you can rest assured, Mr. Doc Dalton, that you will most certainly die here today. I, the great demon Zartrog, will see to that. And I will suck your soul from your dying corpse and take it with me back to Hell. This act will make me famous among all in Hell, and I will be named one of the greatest demons of all time."

The horrible pile of undulating flesh began to pulsate, and several dozen long tentacles slithered toward Dalton. They raised upward like cobras, swaying inches from his face and body. Dalton knew within a few seconds, they would all strike simultaneously, and his soul would be sucked from his body and fast-tracked to Hell.

Dalton was simultaneously frustrated about his situation and embarrassed by his stupidity. How could he have been so easily tricked? He wished he could move his hands just enough to use his weapons. If Dalton was going to die, he wanted to go down fighting, but that most noble death would not be afforded him this day. He was unable to move, was freezing to death, and several dozen snake-like soul-sucking tentacles were about to attack him. His death was imminent, and Dalton imagined the only thing that might have a chance of helping him survive was a storm of circular saw blades that would rain down upon the room and tear these monstrosities to pieces.

No sooner had the thought crossed his mind than Dalton felt his wedding ring begin to pulsate. Within the span of a few milliseconds, several things happened simultaneously. Warmth rapidly flowed from his left hand, up his arm, and throughout his body. The deadly gripping frost began to leave his body. He felt himself sliding down the wall, his feet planting back onto the floor. Then he suddenly heard a buzzing noise that sounded like a thousand angry hornets after someone had smashed their nest.

The room was overrun with countless spinning circular blades, appearing to come from every direction with a ferocity Dalton could scarcely comprehend. The discs appeared to be formed from ice and were no more than three inches in diameter, but they each were equipped with hundreds of razor-sharp gleaming teeth around their circumference. Despite the incredible number of ice blades buzzing about the confined space, none ever collided with another, as if to suggest they might be living sentient beings rather than mechanisms. Whatever their nature, these blades formed a chaotic whirlwind of deadly spinning ice, attacking everything in the room except Dalton.

He stood silently watching as fleshy tentacles and slimy, indistinguishable body parts were turned to mince meat in seconds. The ice clinging to the wall and floor was crushed and chopped, flying in every direction. As the blades finished their work, they exploded into tiny fragments, which immediately melted, forming crimson puddles.

Dalton was equally splattered with gallons of biological gore consisting of blood, slime, melted ice, and demonic flesh fragments. Zartrog scarcely managed to issue a single cry of pain before he was chopped into tiny pieces like lettuce through a food processor. Dalton couldn't help but notice how the shredded remnants on the bed resembled a giant cherry snowcone and knew that particular treat would likely be gone from his diet from now on.

Off to his right, Dalton heard someone scream, "Nooooo," and turned in time to see the minion; Wilbur diced into more miniature fragments than anyone could attempt to count. Then, the mess of shredded flesh and melting blades slid to the floor in a stinking pile of goo.

Less than a minute after the carnage had started, it was over. In the wake of the turmoil, the bedroom looked like a charnel house hit by a hurricane. There wasn't a square inch in the room that wasn't covered and dripping with gore, Dalton included. He waded through several inches of spongy once-human/demonic debris as thick as swamp mud. Several times before he reached the doorway, Dalton could feel his boots almost being sucked off his feet by the disgusting bio-sludge.

Once out in the hallway, Dalton closed the bedroom door, which was no easy task as the sea of revulsion leaked into the hall. It pressed against the door, resisting Dalton's closing force, but eventually, he got the door to shut. A steady, slow flow of thick ruby liquid oozed out from the crack between the door and the floor, but there was little Dalton could do about that.

He had to get home, and Dalton knew he couldn't leave the building and walk down the street in broad daylight looking as revolting as he presently did. He walked along the hallway until he found the bathroom.

It was a large, luxurious place with white tiled walls and floors, upon which Dalton now dripped a continuous barrage of crimson slime. Across the room, Dalton saw a large, glass-enclosed shower. Still dressed from head to toe, he opened the shower door, stepped inside, and turned on the hot water. He knew he would get a proper shower without his clothing once he returned home, but for now, he had to remove the gore from his outerwear as quickly and efficiently as possible.

He didn't want to be in the house any longer than was necessary, so he finished his cleanup quickly and stepped out of the shower, checking his reflection in a nearby full-length mirror. Although resembling an extremely large drowned rat, Dalton was satisfied he had gotten most of the demonic and human waste off his clothing. He left the brownstone, shut the door behind him, and walked home. Fortunately, he encountered few people along the way, and those he did gave him a wide birth, obviously wanting to be far away from this strange, soaking-wet character.

CHAPTER 32

Dalton sat in his favorite recliner in his living room, staring at a 17th-century woodcarving Master Chang had hung there many years earlier. It depicted a scene of a man dressed in a long cloak wielding a sword, battling a hideous demonic creature. The man wore a skull-shaped amulet around his neck. The carving was crude, and many of its elements were indeterminate, but Dalton knew the amulet shown in this carving was the same one he now wore.

With the latest crisis over and after yet another long, therapeutic shower, Dalton finally felt as though he could relax enough to think further about the most recent attack he had just survived. Never before had he encountered demons like those he had to deal with in the past week. He unconsciously twisted his wedding band and thought, had it not been for that strange man in white in the diner bestowing special powers on him through his ring, he would never have survived the week.

As painful a thought as that was for him to consider, it was most definitely true. He couldn't wrap his head around why these attacks were happening now. He had been destroying demons for a decade, and although he had many close calls, the scenarios were always essentially the same. The demons that emerged from the Earth produced lots of fire and attacked him; he retaliated and destroyed them.

But this past week was different. First, Dalton had encountered the doppelganger demon that he had barely managed to outsmart. Next, the strange man in white stopped time and gave him special powers. Then he met that Drabzat demon and destroyed it using his new powers to freeze the monster. During that battle with Drabzat, he had even seen the other medallion briefly, the evil one, before it vanished. Then, finally, he had to deal with the blob demon and its human minion by cutting it to pieces with the spinning ice circular saw blades.

Dalton had dealt with so many new and deadly encounters that had confronted him in just a few days. Something had changed in Dalton's world, something so unimaginable that he was becoming concerned for the first time in years. If the attacks continued to come in increasingly deadly ways, how long would it be before he could no longer successfully fight these creatures? What would happen then?

But he did have the new ring powers and had no idea what their limitations might be. It was true that the two times he had called on these new powers, they had taken the form of cold and ice, but he didn't think that was all they could produce. He suspected that if he needed fire, he would have fire and water if he needed water. Dalton realized that since he had already managed to use these powers, having no idea what he was doing, just imagine how strong he would be once he figured out what the limits to those abilities might be. Perhaps in the right hands, they might be limitless. He didn't know. Hopefully, he could stay alive long enough to find out.

One variable in this equation he still didn't know how to deal with was the other amulet, the evil one. It was in the hands of a powerful, high-level demon, R. John Showalter. Then Dalton realized that was probably why so many new demons had attacked him in the last several days. It had to be Showalter and his accursed medallion. Yes, that seemed to make sense. Showalter had come up from the bowels of Hell to kill Dalton. That was why the attacks had gotten progressively more severe. And that was why the forces of good had sent the white angel, assuming he was some type of angel. Then, his beloved Andrea had been allowed to warn him about the other amulet. They must have known Showalter had returned.

But what could Dalton hope to do against a high-level demon who possessed a medallion with as much, if not more, power than his own? He didn't even know what human form the demon had taken or where the creature lived. Dalton wouldn't recognize Showalter if he tripped over him. And even if he did know who he was and what the man looked like, what good would it do him?

The evil amulet could open doorways to Hell in one location and then close them only to reopen to another location. If Dalton understood how that medallion worked, Showalter could be anywhere in the world one minute and a minute later, wherever else he chose to be. As far as Dalton knew, there was no way to track the demon. He would have to wait until Showalter attacked again, either through one of his underlings or if he chose to attack Dalton himself. If that were to happen, Dalton was apprehensive that he might not survive such an attack.

CHAPTER 33

The demon R. John Showalter sat behind his desk, staring into space, his hands teepeed before him. He was a demon with troubles, and this feeling was both new and uncomfortable for him. He had already invested too much time, energy, and too many demons trying to acquire the soul of that one ridiculous human, Doc Dalton. So far, Dalton had survived everything Showalter had thrown at him. Showalter believed that had that white angelic pest not interfered, his minions would have already made short work of Dalton as he was a mere human. Showalter had access to many of the most powerful demons in Hell. Yet Doc Dalton still lived. What was it about this man that made him so hard to kill?

Showalter wondered if perhaps he would have no choice but to go after Dalton himself. Although it had been centuries since he had needed to get his hands dirty in such a way, maybe he would have no choice. Then an idea came to him. What if, instead of trying to kill Dalton outright, he destroyed everything on Earth that mattered to the man? Perhaps if he couldn't kill Dalton himself, he could crush his spirit and shatter his will to live. Such an attack would have to be carefully planned and carried out to weaken Dalton's spirit, making him more vulnerable to attack.

Dalton had a favorite diner he frequented daily for his breakfast. Showalter had found this out through that worthless human, Wilbur Fernwood, who he had used to lure Dalton to the brownstone. Dalton loved that diner, which meant Showalter had to destroy it and do so in a manner so savage and brutal that the demon hunter would know who was responsible. A waitress who worked in the diner with Dalton was someone with whom Dalton was friendly. Showalter would find a way to use her as well.

Then there was that other place, the one Dalton frequented late at night. What was it called? Max's was its name. Showalter knew Dalton thought fondly of the convenience store and the young man who worked the night shift. Showalter would get a certain morbid pleasure from murdering the man with the inappropriate name, Carlos DeJesus. That store, too, would prove to be an excellent target.

Next, Showalter had to take some time to decide the best and most effective way to carry out his strategy. After a while, he smiled his hideous grin, knowing he had agreed on how and when to put his plan into action. He chuckled to himself, thinking of the horror he would bring to the city that night, a terror so great no one could anticipate its coming. Only one person would understand its origin, and with any luck, it would send Doc Dalton into an uncontrollable rage, which is exactly what Showalter wanted.

CHAPTER 34

The acting clerk, Jose Martinez, sat on a stool with the evening newspaper spread out on the counter. It was a slow evening at Max's convenience store, and the clock had just passed 1:00 AM. Jose was Carlos DeJesus' friend who had stopped by for some cigarettes. Carlos asked him to watch the store so he could go out and get some air. Jose had done this on occasion and knew how everything worked. He was unaware of the violence that had taken place several nights earlier, as not a trace of any disruption could be found. Carlos' "friends" were a very effective cleanup crew. Carlos realized how fortunate he had been that Doc Dalton had been in the store that night. Although he believed he could have taken out the two would-be robbers on his own, Carlos wouldn't have been able to guarantee he could survive such an encounter without incurring some injury. Dalton's presence took care of that.

As Jose read the local news, he heard the familiar albeit annoying sound of the buzzer, signaling the arrival of a customer. Jose looked up to see an old bald man walk slowly across the threshold as the door closed behind him. If there were ever a man for whom the description "unthreatening" was created, this would be that man. Jose had never seen the man before and suspected he might be new to the neighborhood since Jose knew just about everybody. He certainly would have remembered any character that looked like this old gringo.

He wore a brightly patterned Hawaiian shirt that seemed a few sizes too large for his frail, thin body. Likewise, the man's tan cargo shorts looked strange, with his stick-like legs poking out from them. The man wore two socks of different colors and sandals. He walked with the aid of a cane that looked incorrectly adjusted and too tall for his twisted and bent stature. All in all, the old timer was a sad and pitiful sight. The man made his way to the counter and smiled at Jose with a grin that had seen better days, judging by the collection of missing and rotten teeth.

Using his best helpful clerk voice, Jose asked, "Can I help you find something, sir?" He smiled back at the old man, doing his best not to laugh at the funny-looking old timer's large nose and ears, both of which sprouted an abundance of whispy, white hairs that matched his bushy eyebrows. The man didn't sport a beard or mustache, but it was obvious by his gray stubble that he hadn't shaved in several days.

The man grinned stupidly for a few more seconds, then replied, "Are you Carlos DeJesus, also known as C.J. the DJ?".

Had he still been in the store, Carlos might have been flattered that someone knew of his reputation as a party DJ, but Jose suddenly felt uncomfortable being asked about Carlos by such an incredibly odd little old man.

"Carlos ain't here tonight, man. I'm fillin' in for him."

The old man looked at Jose with confusion. "But I was told Carlos would be here. And I know my source to be accurate."

"Sorry, Dude. But like I said, he ain't here."

The old man hesitated, then said, "Oh, my. This is a problem."

Jose said, "It ain't no problem, man. Carlos ain't here, so you might as well hit the road, you know, vamoose."

"Well, here's my dilemma, young man. I don't believe you. In fact, I'm quite certain you are Carlos DeJesus. Therefore, you are the one I have been sent here to see."

"Look, old-timer. I told you Carlos ain't . . ."

Before Jose could finish his sentence, the old man waved his hand dismissively, and Jose stood frozen, paralyzed and unable to speak.

The old man said calmly, "You know, Carlos. Had you simply admitted who you were and not lied, things might have gone a bit better for you. Or perhaps I should say it might have been less painful for you. But what fun would that be? However, now you have managed to anger me, which I must say was a very bad thing to do."

Jose stood in his paralytic state, staring in terror as the strange old man began to change. His former frail body grew in size and musculature until he was so large he stood hunched over, his massive back splitting the ceiling above him. His face had changed into a horror mask of bulging eyes, a pig-like snout, and a wide mouth full of deadly fangs. His giant, ram-like horns ripped plaster from the ceiling as he swung his head to and fro. The creature that had once appeared as a man opened its massive maw and, in one bite, separated Jose's head from his body. It swallowed the head like an old woman enjoying a coconut bon-bon with a look of euphoria on its hideous face as blood trickled down its lips from between its teeth.

Jose's body fell to the floor behind the counter with a thud as blood puddled around his mangled neck stump. The demon turned to look toward the back of the store, raised its long-fingered, clawed hand, and shot molten lava flames from its fingertips like napalm. The liquid fire engulfed the store's interior, and soon, the place became an inferno.

"Hey! What the . . ." A voice cried from the doorway. It was Carlos returning to the store. He couldn't believe his eyes. His store was a mass of swirling flames. But the worst sight was what he witnessed in the middle of the inferno. There was some sort of monster, some giant demon, shooting liquid-like flames from his fingertips resembling a living flamethrower. Carlos stopped in his tracks, and his fight-or-flight instinct kicked into full gear. Being a child of the streets, Carlos had learned this lesson at a very young age. As such, he ran.

Hearing the sound, the creature turned and, without taking time to aim, shot a bolt of fire in the direction of the sound of the voice. Carlos saw the fireball coming his way and dove to the pavement as the flaming orb destroyed the front door of the mini-mart, taking with it the infernally annoying buzzer. Carlos felt heat on the right side of his neck and slapped the fire away as he crawled on his hands and knees as quickly as possible to escape the flaming inferno. When he got around the corner, Carlos got to his feet and ran for all he was worth, never looking back at the fiery Hell that had once been his main place of employment. Although he worried about Jose, his heart was sick, knowing there would be no chance his friend could have survived.

CHAPTER 35

Agnes McDonald walked into the diner promptly at 3:55 A.M. as she had done daily for the past twenty-plus years. Her shift ran from 4:00 A.M. until noon. She loved the breakfast shift. She had once tried the late-night shift for a while but found it too strange. Far too many freaks were walking around the city at night, and most seemed to find their way into her diner. She preferred the breakfast crowd. A few oddballs might show up occasionally, but most of the customers were normal working folks getting some sustenance before starting their days.

She also looked forward to seeing that handsome hunk, Doc Dalton, daily. Even though Agnes knew he and she would never be a couple, she did enjoy their bantering. Agnes was aware Doc was still mourning the loss of his beloved wife more than a decade after her death, and she thought that was something truly special. She had been with many men in her life, including several she had married and divorced, and she could appreciate what it took to have a love like Doc and his wife must have had.

Agnes realized that although she had known Dalton for many years, she knew very little about him. She often wondered what Doc did with his time. Agnes didn't think he had a real job like most people and suspected he might not work at all. He always dressed in an unusual style, looking like some sort of comic book superhero, but she had to admit she found that interesting and a bit mysterious. Most remarkable of all was the skull-shaped medallion Doc wore around his neck. He did his best to ensure it was not visible, but occasionally, she had seen glimpses of the ruby-eyed thing with its strange etchings. Agnes also suspected Doc had various weapons under his long leather coat but never asked about them. This seemed to add to his air of mystery. He was generally closed-mouth about his personal life, and Agnes had no problem with that either. She enjoyed the quirky back-and-forth sexual teasing they had between each other, although she had to admit she was more responsible for it than Doc was. Agnes genuinely liked Doc and considered him a friend. It was unusual for her to have a male friend. She also suspected he felt the same friendship toward her, and if that was all they ever had, she was ok with it.

Agnes looked around the diner, happy to see several familiar faces. The place was already about half full, and she knew little seating would be available within the next few hours. She placed a small "Reserved" card on the seat at the counter that she always saved for Doc. He would likely arrive around his normal time, between six and seven. In the meantime, she had plenty of other customers who needed her attention.

As Agnes stood behind the counter, the door of the diner flew open, and three men dressed in black burst in with guns drawn. They wore black ski masks to hide their faces. The man in the front of the group shouted, "Nobody move. This is a robbery. Remain still and hand over your wallets and jewelry, and nobody will get hurt."

They approached the counter next to the cash register where Agnes stood and said," Open the drawer and give me all the money inside."

Agnes said, "Sure thing. No problem, boys. But I have to tell you that your timing sucks, big time. We already took the night receipts to the bank and are just starting the breakfast shift. That means there ain't much money in here."

The robber had a strange look in his eyes, visible through his facemask. He raised his pistol and pointed it directly at Agnes' face, saying, "You better be wrong about that, sister, or your brains are gonna be decorating that mirror behind you."

Agnes chose not to speak, certain that whatever she said would result in her taking a bullet to the brain. Suddenly, the front door opened, and a middle-aged black-haired man in a dark business suit, blood-red tie, and sunglasses strolled casually inside. The three gunmen turned as one, training all three of their weapons on the man. Agnes noticed a strange skull amulet hanging from the stranger's neck, much like the one Doc Dalton wore, but without the unusual etchings.

One of the gunmen shouted, "Don't move, loser, or you're a dead man."

"Dead man, am I? If you only knew how ironic that statement was," the man replied as he smiled and remained surprisingly calm despite the three guns pointed at him. "Gentleman, it appears you have chosen a blatantly inopportune time to execute this little exercise of yours."

The lead robber looked back at Agnes in confusion as if he did not comprehend what the strange man had said. She translated and explained, "He said that your timing sucks, big time."

"We'll see about that," the robber said as he returned to face the new arrival. Before the gunman could shoot, he saw the air before him shimmer and ripple like a still pond after a pebble had been dropped into it. Then, at the center of the rippling air, a long, oval opening appeared vertically, stretching from the floor to about seven or eight feet in the air. A sickening stench of sulfur, feces, and dead, rotting meat poured from the opening. All three would-be robbers stared in shocked amazement at the impossible site unfolding before them. All the diner customers were equally stunned by the never-before-seen or imagined spectacle.

From the center of the void, a strange screaming came, like the sound of the pain and agony of a million tortured souls all crying out in simultaneous despair. Then, as the three robbers watched in disbelief, more than a dozen long, monstrous, flaming tentacles emerged from the center of the giant vertical opening and wrapped themselves around the men. Wherever the serpentine creatures grabbed onto the men, they instantly burned through clothing and flesh, leaving them to grip bare bones as their victims screamed in agony.

When the tentacles had sufficient grip, they pulled the men in toward the slit in the air, obviously intent on dragging them into whatever horror awaited on the other side. As each robber was dragged screaming into the void, as their flesh came in contact with the flaming sides of the slit, it was flayed from their bodies, liquefied, and subsequently sucked inside. Within seconds, all three villains were gone. The diner was filled with a stench so vile most of the customers were sickened to the point of vomiting. Many had passed out as well.

Agnes somehow managed to stay on her feet and not succumb to the reek that permeated the diner. The horrible portal still hung in the air next to the strange man in the suit, who stood calmly, unaffected by the carnage that had just occurred. He looked directly at Agnes, and she found herself walking out from behind the counter and toward the man. It was like she had no will of her own and could do nothing to stop herself.

"You are Agnes, are you not?" The strange man asked. However, the words didn't travel from his lips to her ears but from his mind to hers. She didn't need to reply as she knew the man, if he was indeed a man, had acquired his answer without the need for her cooperation. Then she heard him say, "Watch now, Agnes, and be horrified."

No sooner had the words appeared in her mind than the stinking slot in the air began to widen, and Agnes saw two slimy, clawed hands gripping the sides, opening the portal wider to make room for it to come through. Now the customers were all screaming and crying and had huddled together near the street side of the diner. A few were trying to smash the windows to escape. Agnes knew there was a back entrance behind the kitchen, but to get there, the people would have to cross in front of the flaming portal, which none would consider. Besides, they were all in shock not only from what had happened to the robbers but from the hideous creature that had emerged from the slit in the air.

It was some type of monster or demon, the likes of which they had never seen in even the most horrid horror movies. The beast stood more than ten feet tall, and its grayish-brown colored flesh was coated with a slimy gel that rippled the air beneath blue, yellow, and red flames. The monster had to hunch under the diner's ceiling because of the size of its massive frame, which rippled with vein-covered bulging muscles. The thing's mouth was large and wide, displaying multiple rows of shark-like teeth and two sets of foot-long tusks extending from its upper and lower jaws. Fiery liquid snot dribbled from its hog-like snout, and its beady piggy eyes glared at the trembling patrons with hatred. The creature turned to look back at the man in the suit as its massive horns tore gouges in the diner ceiling, showering the place in plaster dust as electrical wires sparked and lights flickered. The man simply nodded once in approval, and then all Hell broke loose.

As the man led Agnes out of the diner, she could hear the creature's roar and the agonizing screams of her former customers. The man stopped and turned her so she could have a better view of the diner, now in flames, as the patrons were torn to pieces by the demon within.

As the man led Agnes away, he said, "Dear Agnes. Please allow me to introduce myself. I am R. John Showalter, and you will be my guest for a while. Oh, I can see you don't quite understand what's happening. Not to worry, my dear. I'll try to keep my explanation simple. You are bate. I have destroyed your diner and another place near and dear to a thorn in my side named

Doc Dalton. This act should infuriate Dalton, especially when he learns I killed his friend, Carlos, as well. But I still needed something to push him over the edge and bring him to me. What better than his special lady friend, you, Agnes?"

Agnes was terrified. Not only did she fear for her own life, but now she feared for the life of her friend Doc Dalton. What was it about Doc that such a creature as this would want to harm him? And what sort of man or demon was this? If this horrible creature unleashed those unimaginable monsters against Doc, how could he hope to survive? If Doc died trying to save her, Agnes didn't think she could live with the guilt.

CHAPTER 36

Doc Dalton awoke suddenly at 1:15 A.M., sitting bolt upright in bed. Something was wrong. His skull medallion throbbed against his chest. His wedding ring pulsed on his finger. This was impossible. No demon could pass his security and enter his protected apartment. None of Hell's servants could even know the place existed. Yet his warning devices were telling him something was very wrong. Then, a thought appeared in his mind. He saw a mental image of Max's mini-mart and his friend C.J. engulfed in flames. Dalton didn't know how this image had awoken him, but he understood the vision he had just seen had occurred while he slept.

He jumped out of bed, dressed, and ensured all his weapons were ready to go, then he raced out onto the street and ran the few blocks to Max's. As he got close, Doc saw fire trucks, ambulances, and rescue units blocking the street at Max's. Flames shot outward from the place, and he knew whoever was inside could never have survived. His stomach turned at the apparent loss of his friend.

"Doc? Is that you, Doc?" He heard a voice call from the alley behind him.

Dalton spun around quickly with his two Katana blades already drawn and ready for action. However, no demon or other such threat emerged from the alley. Instead, he saw his friend, C.J., battered but unbroken, limping toward him.

"C.J.? Oh my God, man! I thought you were in there. I thought you were dead. Thank God you escaped," Dalton said.

But C.J. stood looking heartbroken, shaking his head, and said, "I was supposed to be in there, Doc. It was supposed to be me burning in there, but Jose took over for me so I could take a break."

Dalton said, "Oh, man. Not Jose Martinez, Bro. He was good people. What the Hell happened, Carlos?"

Carlos hesitated, then said, "I want to tell you, Doc, but I don't think you'll believe me. Hell, I hardly believe it myself."

Dalton suspected where this discussion was heading and said, "Trust me, C.J., I have seen things in my life most people would would never believe."

"Doc, there was some sort of monster in the store. It was freakin' huge with horns and fingers that shot flames. Do you believe me, Doc?"

"Of course, I believe you, C.J., even though you are right that no one else will."

"But why, Doc. Why do you believe me and not think maybe I'm nuts or something?"

Dalton hesitated, then said, "Do you know what I am, C.J.? Do you know what I do?"

"No, man. I just figured you were cool and not someone to screw with."

"I'll get to that in a moment. So tell me what you saw, C.J."

Carlos hesitated, then said, "There was this thing, this giant monster that shot fire from its fingers. It killed Jose and burned the store."

"That monster you saw was a demon sent from Hell. I have seen many of them in my life. You see, I'm a demon hunter. I hunt and kill those things," Dalton said matter-of-factly.

"A demon? You mean a real demon for Hell? And you say you're a demon hunter? All of a sudden, I ain't sounding so crazy,

136   THOMAS M. MALAFARINA

and that's pretty scary, all things considered," Carlos replied, shaking his head.

"Yeah, I know it's a lot to take in," Dalton agreed.

"Why would some ugly-ass demon from Hell care about me, Doc? It ain't like I was sacrificing chickens in the back room or any weird crap like that. Why me? And why destroy the store?"

Dalton sighed and said, "That's on me, C.J., because I like coming to your store, and you're my friend. That's why you were targeted. The demon that's trying to kill me decided to use you to piss me off, and he succeeded."

"Yeah, well, he managed to piss me off pretty good too, Doc. Jose was a good dude. He was helping me out, and I got him killed. Now, I gotta live with that."

"That's not on you, Carlos. It's on me. I mourn Jose as well, but I also have to take responsibility for nearly getting you killed, too."

Jose grabbed the side of his neck and said, "Well, that damned thing almost got me. I got to the store as it was burning the place to the ground, and it saw me. The weird thing is, it seemed to almost recognize me. It shot some flames at me and burned my neck. I managed to get into the ally and run like Hell, man. But I still got this."

Dalton looked at the long streak of burned flesh on C.J.'s neck, and he flashed back to the night he got his scar helping Sensei Chang. He said, "I hate to tell you this, Carlos, but you've been marked."

"Marked. What do you mean marked?"

Dalton pointed to the faded scar running from his right eye to his mouth. He explained, "I got this a decade ago from a demon when I helped an old Chinese man who was battling them. The bad news is even though the demon didn't kill you, he managed to mark you. That means every demon in Hell will know you are marked and that you are someone that, sooner or later, they will have to come for. And if they kill you, they will take your soul to the deepest bowels of Hell for an eternity of torture. I'm so sorry, C.J., but that's my fault too. They marked you because of me."

Carlos thought for a moment, then said, "Well, although the situation most egregiously sucks, I suppose it still beats what happened to poor Jose. At least I'm still alive, and I will still live to fight another day. Maybe I can get some revenge for Jose. I'm no lightweight, Doc; I can handle myself, you know."

Dalton said, "I do, C.J., but dealing with demons takes a lot more than street fighting skills. You have to be trained as I was trained. It's something we can discuss later." Dalton looked at his watch and said, "Look, it's almost 3:00. Here's what I want you to do. Hide here in the alley until 5:00 then meet me at the diner over on 5th. You know the place?"

"Yeah, Doc. I know it."

"Good. Meet me there. We'll grab some breakfast, then go back to my place and develop an action plan, ok?"

"Ok. But what if one of those demons comes after me?"

Dalton said, "I don't think they will anymore tonight. They were sent to get to me. You should be ok. But if you should smell a bad stink like sulfur or if the ground should crack open and flames shoot out, run."

"Got it. Stink is bad . . . fire is bad . . . running away is good."

Dalton said, "Right. For now, I need you to lie low and meet me at the diner at five. Ok?"

"Ok," C.J. agreed.

Then C.J. vanished into the darkness, as Dalton stood staring at the burning building and the firefighters doing their best to extinguish the flames. He thought about what had happened and decided it had to be the demon Showalter who was doing this to get to him. Since none of the monsters had succeeded in killing Dalton, Showalter must be trying to anger Dalton and throw him off his game. As bad as he felt about Jose, Dalton was happy Carlos had not been killed. As Dalton looked on, he saw rescue workers bringing a body out of the mini-mart on a gurney covered with a sheet, spotted with blood. "Poor Jose," he thought.

Dalton looked at his watch and saw it was 4:30. He hadn't realized how long he had been standing there. It was time to head over to the diner. Then he heard the sound of sirens coming from the direction of 5th Street, and a realization hit him like a ton of bricks. "The diner! Agnes!" Of course. How could he be so stupid as not to realize this might happen? There were two places in the city special to Dalton, and demons had already destroyed one, so it only made sense they would hit the other. Dalton turned and ran toward the diner.

CHAPTER 37

Dalton stood helplessly staring at the flaming ruins of what had once been his favorite place for breakfast. What was worse were the more than two dozen blanket-covered corpses lining the street. Dalton was heartsick. How many innocent souls had been slaughtered needlessly because of him? A fury grew inside him that he feared would soon become beyond his ability to control. He stared at the rows of victims, wondering which of them was his friend, Agnes. He hadn't realized how much the woman had meant to him. The guilt he now felt was not over having feelings for someone besides his beloved Audrey, but because he knew, like with the tragedy at Max's, this disaster too had happened because of him.

As Dalton stared in disbelief and anguish, he felt a light tug on his coat. He looked down and saw a small boy standing next to him. Dalton said, "This is no place for you to be, child. You had better head back to your home."

The boy looked up at the man, who must have looked like a giant to him. He lifted a folded sheet of paper and said, "Are you the one they call Doc Dalton? The man with the dark suit said I should give this to you. He gave me five dollars." The boy smiled sheepishly, handed Dalton the paper, turned, and ran off into the early morning darkness. At first, Dalton was too shocked by what was happening around him and confused by his anger to realize what this was all about. Then he suddenly understood. He walked to a nearby streetlight, unfolded the paper, and read its contents.

The note read, "Good morning, Doc Dalton. How did you like the show I put together for you? Quite impressive, if I must say so myself. Although things didn't go exactly as planned, they seldom do. I really wanted my demon, Garzot, to kill your friend Carlos, but apparently, there was a mixup on his part, for which my minion will be severely punished. However, at least he was able to mark your friend, which will make it much easier for us to recognize him for a future encounter. And believe me, Mr. Dalton, we will be seeing Carlos soon.

"In the meantime, I'm sure your heart is broken worrying about which of those crispy critters lying on the ground is your precious Agnes. Well, you can relax, Doc Dalton. Your lovely lady friend is safe and sound with me. That is to say, safe for now. I'm not sure how long I will decide to keep her safe. I suppose that depends on you. I have a group of several very disgusting and well-endowed demons who can't wait for a chance to have their way with the lady. All I have to do is say the word, and she will be ravaged in ways you could never imagine.

"Here are my instructions for you, Mr. Dalton. That is if you ever wish to see your precious Agnes whole again. I want you to meet me at an abandoned waterfront warehouse at the corner of Water Street and Elm. Be there tonight before sunset, and you might have a chance to save Agnes from excruciating pain beyond imagining. If you are late, I'll give the woman to my minions. I hope you are late as I will enjoy hearing her screams. – R. John Showalter."

Dalton looked at the note and read it again. As he read, his anger grew, and even though he knew he had to control his emotions, his fury seemed to be unstoppable. He had to get to the warehouse and save Agnes. Dalton crumpled the paper, dropped it unconsciously to the ground, and prepared himself for his encounter at the waterfront for what could be his final showdown.

CHAPTER 38

Carlos arrived at the diner precisely at 5:00 A.M. to find the place in flames and dozens of charred bodies covered with bloody, blackened sheets lined up along the street. He looked around for Dalton but couldn't see him anywhere. A man of Dalton's size was not easily hidden, so Carlos had to assume Dalton either hadn't arrived yet or had been there, seen the carnage, and left. But if so, where had he gone?

As Carlos stared in disbelief, two more charred bodies were removed from the diner. The air was redolent with the stench of burning meat. Carlos realized the source of that smell, making his stomach turn. If Doc had been there already, then he too would have seen what Carlos was seeing, and Doc must have been riddled with guilt. He was already suffering with remorse over Jose, so a site like the one Carlos was seeing must have pushed him over the edge.

A sudden gust of wind blew something past Carlos' feet. Carlos bent down and saw a crumpled paper with a note written on it. As Carlos read the note, his fingers trembled with fury. This demon, Showalter, who had written the note, had mentioned Carlos by name and said Hell would eventually come for him. As if that was not bad enough, the monster had destroyed the diner, killed dozens of innocent people, and then kidnapped the waitress, Agnes, and used her as bait to trap Doc. Carlos had no idea if Agnes and Doc were more than friends. Apparently, that didn't matter to this horrible demon, as the creature had already sent monsters to kill Doc in the past.

Carlos felt helpless. Less than five hours earlier, he had no idea that there were even such things as demons in the world. He had heard anecdotes told by his elderly abuela, but as far as Carlos was concerned, they had all been nothing more than stories, fictitious old wives' tales. But everything had changed tonight, and not for the better. He had seen one of the creatures with his own eyes. He had lost a friend to the demon, and he, himself, had nearly been killed. Carlos had been burned, scarred, and labeled for death.

Now, he had just read that not only was he marked as Doc had told him, but he had just been mentioned by the very demon responsible for all the death and destruction and who was after Doc. If anything happened to Doc, Carlos would be on his own to face whatever evil Hell sent to get him. Carlos found himself struggling with many emotions at the same time. He was saddened by the loss of Jose, angered by what had happened, and terrified to learn that he was on Hell's radar with no idea how to defend himself.

Carlos read the note again and saw the meeting place this R. John Showalter demon had given Doc, and he knew what he would have to do, whether he was prepared or not.

CHAPTER 39

Doc Dalton stood at the intersection of Water and Elm Streets, looking carefully in both directions while studying the abandoned warehouse. He had forced his emotions aside so he could return to a state of calm indifference. This was how Dalton had faced and defeated so many demons before. As such, Dalton knew it would be necessary for what he was certain that he was about to face. Even though he had fought and defeated many demons in the past, Dalton suspected he had never encountered a situation as dire as he believed he would face this day.

The streets were empty in both directions, and the warehouse windows were empty sockets that seemed to mock Dalton's very existence. He knew Showalter was watching him from whatever stinking corner of Hell he must be hiding. There was only one way to get things moving, and that was to call the demon out. Dalton shouted into the emptiness, "I am here, Showalter. Show yourself, as I am eager to face and destroy you."

As if in answer to his challenge, the air began to shimmer and ripple simultaneously in three different places: Elm Street, Water Street, and directly in front of the warehouse. Three separate portals appeared in the air, and the familiar sulfur stench of Hell poured forth from them. As if that were not enough to send chills through the souls of any man, the surfaces of Water and

Elm Streets began to rumble and split open, spewing smoke, fire, and molten liquid upward. Dalton knew he was about to face not only a single demonic attack but a multi-pronged onslaught from at least five different places.

Although he was never frightened to do what he was made to do, Dalton was apprehensive regarding his chances of surviving such an attack. He felt his skull pendant vibrate against his chest. His hands rested on the grips of his Katana blades, and Dalton could also feel them tremble with anticipation. Then, he sensed the slow throbbing of his wedding ring and was reminded that he would not be alone in this fight. He had the tools, the strength, the skill, and the courage he needed to defeat the forces of evil. Dalton would have to have faith that he could prevail.

The three vertical portals began to expand at the center, and as they did, from two of them, the most hideous creatures Dalton had ever seen stepped down to the street, waiting for the signal to attack. The one to his left on Elm Street was some type of hideously deformed thing, with a large, bulbous head adorned with more than a dozen pointy spiral horns, a half-dozen bulging eyes, two snot-dripping nostrils, and an enormous fang-filled mouth. It had no torso to speak of but a cluster of several dozen tentacles, some shorter, which supported its wobbling frame while others were longer. The longer tentacles stretched out in anticipation of grabbing their prey. At the ends of these flapping appendages were mouths lined with dozens of rows of pointed teeth. These were similar to those Dalton had faced before, but had never been attached to such a hideous creature.

On the Water Street side portal, another horrible demon awaited. This thing stood on four long legs like those of a camel, but that is where any resemblance to the dromedary ended. The creature atop those legs looked like a mix of a human, a wolf, a spider, and a slug. It had a deformed human-like face, appearing to be in the throes of agony, its mouth hanging open, revealing a mess of broken tombstone teeth. The creature's body was wolf-like and fur-covered, as were the many spider legs that jutted outward, waving frantically in the air. At the ends of those hairy legs, huge eyeballs moved around, probing the area for victims. The creature dragged a long slug-like abdomen behind it, leaving a deadly molten sludge trail. Dalton suspected that tail could be whipped like a scorpion's to shoot a barrage of lethal slime at its intended victims.

At the crevice that had split open in the middle of each street, snake-like tentacle creatures of the kind Dalton had defeated in the past waved in the air like cobras while two troll-like monstrosities emerged from the fire pits. Each monster was over twelve feet tall and carried huge, flaming swords. The naked, muscular, and overly-endowed creatures bore piercings in their flesh of various types, from long rusted pins and nails to barbed wire, razor wire, and concertina wire. It was obvious the monsters had been tortured in the most unimaginable ways. But despite their pain and agony, they were here for one purpose: to kill Dalton. He had no doubt who commanded this make-shift army of the damned.

That was when the center portal opened, and a mass of writhing, slime-coated tentacles spilled out of the bottom, forming themselves into a set of living, pulsating stairs. From the opening stepped a dark-haired man in a black suit, black shirt, and blood-red tie wearing dark sunglasses. He wore a silver skull medallion with glowing ruby eyes, which hung on a silver chain around his neck. Behind him, he pulled a stricken but apparently physically unharmed Agnes out of the void. Dalton could only imagine what sort of Hellish horrors she had been forced to witness inside that portal. He suspected it was a wonder she had not gone mad; at least, he hoped she had not. Judging by her vacant stare, he wasn't so sure.

"Well, good evening, Mr. Dalton. I see I successfully got your attention with my little presentation, and it's equally nice that you got my message. I'd say I apologize for using such extreme measures to get you to notice me, but the truth is, I'm not sorry at all. You see, I rather enjoyed myself. There's something about the sounds of humans screaming and dying in agony that I find incredibly enjoyable. I always say it's personally rewarding to take pleasure in one's responsibilities. Don't you agree?"

Dalton said nothing, choosing instead to analyze the various aspects of his situation further. All around him, demons were in position and eager to attack. Before him stood the dreaded demon master, with Agnes under his control. Dalton knew soon the demon Showalter would give the command to attack. Dalton wanted this braggart from Hell to keep talking for as long as possible so he could anticipate various scenarios and prepare his defense. Dalton knew it wouldn't be enough for him to survive this encounter. He had to destroy the demon, Showalter, and find a way to rescue Agnes.

Showalter said, "What's wrong, Doc? Don't you have anything witty to say in rebuttal, nothing to say in your defense? Now might be a good time to beg for your life, as little good as that might do. Whether you realize it or not, you are going to die this evening. I am going to claim your soul, and you will spend eternity in agonizing torment."

Dalton sensed the two creatures from the portal slowly advancing toward him. He gripped tightly to his Katana blades, never taking his hateful gaze from the hidden eyes of the demon Showalter. The bulbous head demon was approaching from the left, and the slug-tailed creature was coming from the right. Dalton was surprised that the master demon hadn't ordered all the monsters to attack simultaneously. He doubted he could have survived such an onslaught. Perhaps Showalter's strategy was to have him fight the monsters separately to tire Dalton and wear him down. That way, Showalter could have the pleasure of finishing him off.

Whatever the case, Dalton was much happier to see these two demons coming for him while the giant troll-like creatures waited in the wings. He knew battling these creatures individually might have tired another man, but he was not just any other man. He was Doc Dalton, Demon Hunter, and despite his calm demeanor, Dalton was boiling over with energy fueled by rage. He was ready for whatever this minion of Hell had to throw at him.

As Dalton waited for the demons to get close enough for his attack, Showalter led Agnes off the slimy tentacled stairs, and seconds later, the fleshy creatures arose and formed a cage around Agnes. Dalton knew the power of those snake-like creatures. If Agnes accidentally touched their slimy skin, they would burn her flesh away. If the creatures closed in on Agnes, she would scream in agonizing terror as the flesh melted from her skeleton, leaving a skinless pile of bones in their wake. This was another obstacle Dalton would have to deal with later, but first things first.

The bulbous-headed creature reached out with its octopodal arms, its razor-sharp teeth chomping in anticipation of tasting Dalton. From the right, the other creature raised its slug-like tail over its furry body, intending to coat Dalton with its napalm-like ooze. Dalton drew his blades with lightning speed and sliced off five of the approaching creature's chomping tentacles. Dalton ducked and rolled as the appendages fell to the ground and flopped about before dissolving into a stinking liquid amid the howls of pain from the wounded creature.

The monster on his right released a blast of the flaming substance from its slug-like tail, which coated the bulbous head monster, melting it instantly. Dalton shot forward with his right blade and pierced the human-like face of the second creature. Dalton severed several of the thing's spider-like legs with his left-hand blade. The beast fell over on its back, exposing its underbelly. Dalton was about to cut the thing's head off when a giant blade came down and cut the monster in half. Dalton looked up and saw one of the troll demons who had tried to hit him but missed him and killed the spider creature instead.

Dalton felt the ground tremble as the second troll creature stomped its way over to join the action. The first beast pulled back its scimitars, ready to slice Dalton in two, but before it could swing, Dalton pointed his wedding ring at the demon, and a bolt of ice flew from his ring like a spear and passed through the center of the monster, cleaving it cleanly in two. Dalton turned to face the second demon, but its scimitar was already in motion. Dalton jumped backward and just missed being hit. Unfortunately, the blade cut through the chain holding his skull amulet, which flew through the air and out of sight. Before the demon could swing again, Dalton drove his blade up through the monster's chin and into what passed for its brain. The magic symbols on his blade did their work, and the demon was killed instantly. Dalton turned to face the demon, Showalter.

"Very good, Dalton. You surprised me with how quickly you were able to vanquish my four minions. Unfortunately, now it seems I must face you myself."

Dalton stood straight with his blades ready and said, "Bring it on, demon. I will send you screaming back to Hell."

"Sorry, Dalton. That's not how this is going to work. You are going to lay down your weapons and come to me. You will not resist or try to harm me."

"What makes you think I would ever do such a foolish thing, Showalter?"

The demon looked at the cage of fleshy tentacles, and they began to close in toward the barely conscious Agnes. "Because if you don't do what I say, I will melt the flesh from this piece of human trash you so admire while you watch helpless to do anything."

Dalton didn't know what to do. He couldn't surrender his precious Katana blades to this demon. If he did, Dalton would guarantee his own death. This demon would kill him and send his soul to Hell. But if he didn't, the wretched monster would kill Agness in an agony too brutal to imagine. Dalton hung his head in defeat. He could not let Agnes die because of him. Dalton threw his blade down to the ground with a frustrated sigh.

CHAPTER 40

Carlos DeJesus stood in the shadows, watching the battle at the intersections of Water and Elm Streets. He couldn't believe the horrid creatures that had tried to kill Doc. One was more heinous than the next. Carlos watched in amazement as the bulbous-headed octopus creature tried to grab Doc with its tentacles. Carlos watched in awe as Dalton cut off several of the monster's legs. Then Doc rolled out of the way just as the second creature shot some kind of flaming gunk from its tail, accidentally coating the big-headed monster and dissolving it into a blob of bubbling goo in a matter of seconds.

Carlos watched as Doc drove one of his Katana blades into the human head of the second monster while using the other blade to cut off several of the monster's hairy legs. Carlos couldn't believe the speed at which his friend could move. That second creature flipped over on its back and before Doc could kill it, one of the enormous demons that crawled from the fiery pit tried to kill Dalton with its flaming sword. The troll creature's giant sword came down on the hairy creature's abdomen, cleaving the beast in half.

The demon recovered from its mistake and stood tall with its two flaming scimitars ready to slice Doc. Then something incredible happened. Dalton raised his left hand, pointing a fist at the demon, and a giant spear of what looked like ice flew out of Doc's wedding ring. How the Hell had Doc managed to do such an incredible thing? The monster was cut neatly in half. Carlos then saw Doc turn to face the second demon, which was charging like a wild bull, swinging its sword like a battle ax. Dalton jumped back in time, barely missing and being sliced in half. Carlos saw the demon's blade cut through the chain, holding Dalton's skull medallion and sending it through the air. Then Dalton drove his blade up through the monster's chin, killing the beast.

Carlos followed the trajectory of the amulet as it landed in a pile of debris. He crawled on his hands and knees toward where the medallion landed, doing his best not to be seen. Carlos knew he had to recover the amulet for his friend. He didn't know if he could get it back to Doc without getting killed himself, and he didn't know if doing so could even help his friend, but Carlos believed he had to try.

As Carlos crept closer, he saw Agnes confined in a cage constructed of numerous worm-like creatures with slime-coated flaming flesh. Agnes seemed to be in a state of hypnosis and unable to move or react to what was happening around her. Carlos suspected if Agnes touched those creatures' skin, she would be burned to death. He had to find some way to help Doc destroy the demon, Showalter, and set Agnes free. But what could he hope to do? He was just a young man with no superpowers. Carlos only had street smarts, which likely wouldn't help him in this situation.

Carlos heard the demon order Doc to lay down his weapons. He threatened to burn Agnes alive if Doc didn't do as he commanded. Carlos waited, certain that Doc must have some trick up his sleeve. He had just seen Doc shoot an icy spear from the ring on his left hand. Surely, Doc might be able to do something to neutralize the cage creatures and eliminate the danger to Agnes. Then Carlos realized that Doc wouldn't want to risk harming Agnes while trying to save her. It looked like the only hope left for Doc Dalton lay in Carlos' hands.

Suddenly, Carlos felt a vibration and looked down to see the skull medallion he held, which seemed to be alive. Its silver essence glowed brightly, and the various etchings on its surface turned a luminous blue as a cerulean light flowed along the path formed by the connecting glyphs. Then the ruby eyes glowed so brightly, Carlos could scarcely look at them. An idea appeared in his mind, and despite his fear and uncertainty, Carlos understood what he needed to do.

CHAPTER 41

Dalton stood with his head down, no more than ten feet from the demon master, knowing he would most certainly be killed at any moment. He said, "I have done what you asked, Showalter. I will surrender myself to you if you will let Agnes go."

The demon laughed, saying, "I cannot believe how gullible you humans are. Your ignorance never ceases to amaze me. Do you honestly believe you can stand there, utterly defenseless, and bargain with me? I don't make deals, Doc Dalton. This sow you call Agnes is mine to do with as I please, no matter what you request. Likewise, you are now mine, as is your immortal soul."

Then the demon pointed his finger at Dalton, and the big man was forced to his knees, helpless to defend himself. He had tried to bring forth some power from his wedding ring but couldn't seem to do so. He looked up and saw the amulet hung around Showalter's neck, glowing as brightly as its ruby eyes. Dalton realized it was that evil medallion that was suppressing his ability to use his new power. He grabbed for his own amulet and realized it was gone.

The demon now pointed both hands at Dalton, and the big man began to tremble, writhing in pain as he felt his life force leaving his body. Dalton knew he was dying and that now he would never get to be with his precious Audrey again.

Showalter shouted, "You are defeated, Doc Dalton, and now your soul will be mine."

A voice shouted from the shadows, "Not so fast, pendejo. That's my friend you're screwin' with, and I don't like people messin' with the Doc."

The demon turned and saw what appeared to be some street punk running out of the darkness. Carlos had no idea if what he was about to do would work, but he had no choice. Showalter shouted, "Then, you will join your friend." Before the demon could react, Carlos hurled the skull amulet with all his might.

The medallion flew directly to the evil skull medallion as if drawn by some incredible magnetic force. The two skulls came together face to face with a crash of thunder and white-hot lightning. Carlos heard Showalter scream as his power over Dalton was cut off. Dalton staggered to his feet as the demon shrieked in agony.

"Stand back, C.J., this is gonna be bad."

"You ain't gonna have to tell me twice," Carlos shouted as he dove behind the debris pile.

Dalton decided he wouldn't take any chances as he pointed his ring toward the demon. Suddenly, an incredible blast of white energy shot from his ring, forming an enormous semicircular dome between Dalton, Carlos, and the evil demon. Through the transparent shield, Dawson saw the demon change. Showalter's sunglasses flew from his face, revealing two bulging eyes that seemed to pop out of his skull. Long, ram-like horns jutted from his forehead, bending back along his head. His skin changed, becoming greenish-gray as his nose pulled back into a pig-like snout. As the demon screamed in his death throes, his mouth became huge with layers of fangs.

Before Dalton could make out more of the creature that only moments earlier appeared human, the demon began to break down into millions of gray-black particles like a newspaper burning in a fire pit. This was followed by an ear-splitting blast that shook the abandoned warehouse, causing it to collapse to the ground in a booming pile of rubble and a giant cloud of dust.

When the dust settled, Dalton saw a pile of burned ash lying where the demon Showalter once stood. He looked over to Agnes and saw the creatures that had held her captive were gone, and she was sitting on the ground, obviously in shock. She was covered in dirt and grime and looked shell-shocked, like someone who had just survived a bombing, which Dalton supposed she had.

Amid the dust, Dalton saw the gleam of silver and bent down to retrieve his amulet. He was surprised to find it was in perfect condition, looking as new as it had moments earlier, its protective glyphs visible and unharmed.

"Is the medallion ok, Doc?" Carlos asked.

"Yes. It looks as good as new," he replied.

Then Carlos asked, "What about the other one? The one that demon wore?"

Dalton looked around and kicked aside the ashes that were all that was left of the demon master. "I don't see it anywhere."

"Do you think it was destroyed, Doc?"

Dalton looked down at the ground, shook his head, and said, "I don't know, C.J. I suppose it's possible that my medallion destroyed it, but it's equally as likely that it sent the accursed thing back into Hell. I suppose I'll never know."

Carlos said, "Well, all I can do is hope you're right, Doc. I sure don't want to ever encounter that thing again."

"One thing I can always be certain of, C.J., is that I can't be certain of anything."

Carlos asked, "What are we gonna do now, Doc? We have to get out of here before somebody reports an explosion and building collapse. And we need to take care of Agnes."

Dalton said, "Here's what I want you to do, C.J. I need you to get Agnes to the hospital. It's only a few blocks from here. Tell them who she is and say you know her from the diner that burned down this morning. You suspect she has been wandering around in a stupor all day. Tell them you found her, and she seems to be non-responsive and needs medical attention."

"What are you going to do, Doc?" Carlos asked.

"I'm going back home and think about what happened here today. I don't know if you realize it or not, C.J., but your quick thinking saved my life. What you also probably don't realize is that you're a natural at this demon-hunting stuff."

"I am? How do you know?"

"I know because someone once said the same thing to me long ago, and he was right, as I'm sure I am."

Doc handed Carlos a blank black business card containing simply a phone number. After you get help for Agnes, go home and try to rest. Call me tomorrow, and we can meet to talk about the future. As you may have already assumed, we have much to discuss."

CHAPTER 42

Dalton waited near Agnes' bedside for her to wake up. It had been a long two weeks that she lay in her hospital bed in a catatonic state. Her doctors had done all they could to help her. Now, her fate was out of their hands. Carlos had done as Dalton had requested and had gotten Agnes safely to the hospital. Since Agnes had worked at the diner for so many years, the police believed the story that Carlos had found her roaming the neighborhood in a stupor. Half of the police and firemen were practically in shock themselves over the diner tragedy; so much sorrow, so many deaths.

Apparently, no one associated Carlos with the fire at Max's convenience store because he was never questioned about it. Once he dropped Agnes at the hospital emergency room, he was allowed to leave. It probably helped that he said his name was Julio Rodriguez and that he "*no hables Ingles.*" Carlos later met Dalton, who took him back to his apartment building and set him up with a new place to live.

For the past year, Dalton had occasionally wondered if his demon-hunting activities would end when his life finally ended, but now he knew he would have an apprentice to take over, just as he had done for Sensei Chang. Dalton found it ironic how the very act meant to kill C.J. had resulted in his becoming Dalton's student. He had much to teach the young man, and the training began immediately. Carlos was twenty years younger than Dalton, and although he planned to live for many years to come, Dalton liked the idea of someone being able to pick up where he left off. Dalton felt he was responsible for the young man because Carlos' life had suddenly changed so drastically because of Dalton. Not to mention that Carlos saved Dalton's life and destroyed the evil demon, R. John Showalter and all without a bit of training.

Dalton assumed the evil pendant had survived the battle and was sent back to Hell. He supposed, at some point, the evil amulet would return in the hands of yet another higher-level demon. However, there was little Dalton could do about that other than keep fighting the good fight and prepare himself and Carlos as best as possible for whenever that day came.

As Dalton watched Agnes sleep her unnatural slumber, he noticed her right hand twitch. He had asked the doctors about this when it had happened previously. The doctors would not acknowledge these movements as anything other than involuntary twitches. But Dalton felt there was something different about that twitch. He felt a slight tremble in his skull medallion, which he sensed did not signal something bad but something good was about to occur.

Agnes' eyes fluttered slightly, then opened. She appeared disoriented, as was to be expected. She asked, "Doc? Where am I? Why are you here?"

Dalton offered a concerned smile to his friend and said, "Welcome back, Agnes. How are you feeling?"

Agnes hesitated, then said, "I think I feel fine, Doc. I'm a bit confused, but other than that, I'm okay. Why wouldn't I be?" Agnes looked around and asked, "What is this place? Is this a hospital? What the Hell am I doing in a hospital, Doc?"

Dalton said, "I'll get to that shortly. Tell me, Agnes. What do you remember?"

"Remember? Remember about what?" She said, not understanding.

"What's the last thing you recall, Agnes?"

She thought for a bit, then said, "I remember being at the diner for my shift, and then these three street thugs came in to rob the place. They didn't shoot me, did they, Doc?"

"No, Agnes. You were lucky. Nobody shot you. Do you recall anything else?"

Agnes said, "Nope. That's it. One of the bad guys pointed a gun at me and told me to open the cash register. That's all I remember. What happened?"

Dalton put his concocted story into play and said, "Well, Agnes. We don't know. You were found wandering the streets in a stupor, all covered with grime. A stranger found you and brought you here to the hospital. That was a week ago."

"A week ago? Oh, my Lord! Did I miss a week of work? Bill, the owner will fire me for sure."

Dalton said, "There's more to the story, Agnes. We suspect the three robbers must have knocked you unconscious or something like that. Then, they burned down the diner, killing dozens of customers inside. Somehow, you must have come to and crawled out of the diner. It was a total loss. You were the only survivor."

Agnes was shocked, "What? How could that be? Is everything really gone?"

"Yes, Agnes. It was a total loss. The death toll was thirty-five people. Is that all you remember? Nothing else?"

Agnes thought for a moment, then said, "No, Doc. Nothing else. Have I really been in here for a week?"

"Yes, you have, Agnes. Bill, the diner owner, has been by to check on you several times. He is very concerned about his number one favorite waitress, as am I."

"I can't believe you came to see me, Doc. That's very sweet of you."

Doc grinned and said, "That's me. Just a big old sweetie pie for sure."

Agnes hesitated and said, "I had some really strange dreams, though; really weird dreams."

"Weird, how?" Dalton asked, suddenly concerned.

"Well, really weird dreams with monsters, fire, and stuff like that."

Dalton said, "Wow. That must be some strong medicine they gave you to make that happen."

"Yes. I suppose you're right. They were just so realistic," Agnes said, appearing uncertain.

Agnes' doctor came into the room and looked surprised to see Agnes awake and communicating. He said, "Well, Ms McDonald, it's great to have you back among the living once again. You had us quite concerned for a time."

Dalton looked from the doctor to Agnes, feeling a bit out of place, and then said, "Ok. Doctor. Now that Agnes is awake and recovering, I have to head out for a bit. You be sure to take good care of her, you hear?" Dalton followed that with his patented killer scowl.

"You bet, Mr. Dalton. She's in good hands, as you well know," the doctor replied with a bit of concern in his voice.

As Dalton left the room, heading down the hallway, Agnes asked, "Has he been here to check on me often?"

The doctor replied, obviously relieved to see Dalton go, "Oh yes. Every day . . . for many hours. But nobody was brave enough to ask him to leave. He's quite the insistent sort, you know."

Agnes smiled and said, "Oh yes. I know him very well." Then she got a look of concern and said, "I just realized I don't have health insurance, and my place of employment burned to the ground. How in the name of God am I going to pay this hospital bill?"

The doctor said, "Not to worry, Ms. McDonald. Your medical expenses have all been covered. You have nothing to worry about."

Agnes was stunned, "But how, Doctor? Who did this?"

"Your good but rather frightening friend, Mr. Dalton, took care of everything. You're very lucky to have a friend like him."

Agnes said, "Yes, I am. Before today, I had no idea just how lucky I am to have him."

EPILOGUE

Almost a year had passed since Dalton's near-fatal encounter with the demon Showalter. Max's convenience store had yet to be rebuilt. According to C.J., the owner, Maximillian Padu, was taking his time and deciding if he would be better off opening a new store in a better neighborhood and forgetting about the old location. No matter where Max chose to build, Carlos DeJesus would not be welcome back as an employee. To say he was persona non grata was an understatement. Max had gotten into a great deal of costly legal trouble because of the death of Jose.

Jose had not been an employee of Maximillian's company and, as such, had no business behind the counter. It had been Carlos who asked Jose to fill in for him. This simple request led to Jose's death. Max knew nothing about demons or that such a creature was sent to the store to get Carlos and destroy the market. All Max knew was that the mini-mart had burned down, a non-employee was running the place, and Carlos had not been at his post. Max was being hounded by Jose's relatives, insurance companies, and lawyers. The final result of that fiasco would be bounced around the courts for years to come. Fortunately, other than incurring Max's ire, Carlos had been excluded from all the legal hassles and had been able to spend the year training with Dalton.

The diner where Agnes had worked had been rebuilt and open for its first day of business. She was back on her breakfast shift after being unemployed for the past year. Agnes had gone to her landlord to explain her financial situation, and he told her that her rent had been paid for the next year and that there was nothing to worry about. She asked who had paid her rent, and he said, "I don't know who this fella was, but he sure was a big scary-looking dude, and he gave me a bag of cash, so you're covered." Of course, once again, she knew Dalton had come to her rescue.

As Agnes was busy caring for diner customers, a young Hispanic man entered and sat on the stool next to the one with the "Reserved" sign. She didn't know if Dalton would be in on the diner's reopening day, but if he did come in, she wanted to ensure his seat was available at the counter. This young man was dressed very similarly to the way Doc Dalton dressed. In fact, he looked like a mini-Dalton or a Dalton wannabe.

Then Dalton arrived, and his eyes met Agnes', who was waiting for him at the counter. He walked slowly to his seat, never taking his eyes off the waitress. Agnes smiled and said, "Welcome back, Sweetie. It's been a long time. I understand I owe you more thanks than I can possibly hope to give you."

Doc smiled back, removed the 'Reserved' sign, took a seat, and said, "You don't owe me anything, Agnes. Your smile and a good breakfast are all the thanks I need." Then Dalton winked at her. It was something new, something he had never done before. Agnes felt a familiar pleasant tingle from head to toe.

Agnes pointed at the fellow sitting next to Dalton and said, "So, Doc. Whose the 'Mini-me' over here?"

Dalton chuckled and said, "That's my cohort in crime, C.J. We . . . um . . . let's say . . . work together."

"And what sort of work exactly do you and your new sidekick do? Are you guys like Batman and Robin?" Agnes said, giving her sexiest smile.

Dalton hesitated and said, "Yeah, something like that." There was no way he would tell Agnes any more about his activities than that. Nor would he allow her to get any closer to him than being his waitress and friend. He was thankful she had no memory of what had happened to her or what could have happened had Carlos not come to their aid. Dalton also hoped that when the demon Showalter was destroyed, any knowledge of Agnes being Dalton's friend had died with him. The best way to keep her safe was to keep her distant.

Fortunately, Agnes hadn't been marked as Carlos had, so no demons would know about her. Agnes would be safe if Dalton kept her at arm's length. Dalton was surprised to find that this fact bothered him. During the ordeal a year earlier, Dalton realized he cared for Agnes more than he had known. Unfortunately, he would have to put his feelings aside for her safety.

"So, Doc, what'll it be? The regular?" Agnes asked, still fighting the new and pleasant emotions she was feeling.

"You bet. And bring one for my boy, C.J.," Dalton said.

Agnes said, "You got it, Doc, Honey Pie. One big, strong, hungry-man breakfast coming right up. Oh yeah, and one slightly smaller version for your little buddy." Agnes turned to walk away, shaking her backside for all it was worth.

"Madre María!" Carlos exclaimed, ogling the waitress. "That thang is downright hypnotic."

Dalton said, "Easy, Amigo. That piece of real estate is off-limits to friendly neighborhood Demon Hunters like us."

"True dat!" Carlos agreed.

www.ingramcontent.com/pod-product-compliance
Lightning Source LLC
Chambersburg PA
CBHW020333260626
47156CB00004B/1503